D0542880

3 8028 02231340 4

'Has the cat got your tongue, Cat?' he asked as she stood in silence.

It would seem that it had, because still she said nothing.

'Well, I'll make this very simple for you, then.' He pushed on. 'A, B or C?'

Cat could feel her eyelashes blink rapidly as he sped through the multiple choices he had created just for her.

'Is the baby A—mine, B—not mine, or C—not sure?'

'Dominic...' she said, and how strange it felt to be saying his name while looking at him again. How odd it felt that he was here...terribly beautiful, terribly cross. 'It's not that simple...' Cat attempted.

But it was to him.

'A, B or C, Cat?'

She couldn't meet his eyes as she delivered the answer. 'A.'

'Mine.'

Yours.

His.

Dear Reader,

Some stories write themselves. Not all. Often I'm tearing my hair out. But I wasn't with Cat and Dominic. I actually had a plan with this story…my hero and heroine simply refused to stick to it.

I kept reminding them that *I* was the writer, but they refused to listen and I actually couldn't type fast enough some days to keep up with them. I simply loved them both, and I wanted to get to their happy-ever-after so that I could see for myself how *they* worked things out.

I hope you enjoy meeting them as much as I did.

Happy reading!

Carol x

THE BABY OF
THEIR DREAMS

BY
CAROL MARINELLI

All rights reserved including the right of reproduction in whole
or in part in any form. This edition is published by arrangement with
Harlequin Books S.A.

This is a work of fiction. Names, characters, places, locations and
incidents are purely fictional and bear no relationship to any real
life individuals, living or dead, or to any actual places, business
establishments, locations, events or incidents. Any resemblance is
entirely coincidental.

This book is sold subject to the condition that it shall not, by way of
trade or otherwise, be lent, resold, hired out or otherwise circulated
without the prior consent of the publisher in any form of binding or
cover other than that in which it is published and without a similar
condition including this condition being imposed on the subsequent
purchaser.

® and TM are trademarks owned and used by the trademark owner
and/or its licensee. Trademarks marked with ® are registered with the
United Kingdom Patent Office and/or the Office for Harmonisation in
the Internal Market and in other countries.

First published in Great Britain 2015
by Mills & Boon, an imprint of Harlequin (UK) Limited,
Eton House, 18-24 Paradise Road, Richmond, Surrey, TW9 1SR

© 2015 Carol Marinelli

ISBN: 978-0-263-25900-1

Harlequin (UK) Limited's policy is to use papers that are natural,
renewable and recyclable products and made from wood grown in
sus~~tainable~~   conform
to t~~he~~   ~~n~~.

Pri~~nted~~
by ~~CPI Antony Rowe, Chippenham~~

**GREENWICH
LIBRARIES**

3 8028 02231340 4	
Askews & Holts	30-Sep-2015
AF MAR ROM	£14.50
4790816	AF no.

Carol Marinelli recently filled in a form where she was asked for her job title and was thrilled, after all these years, to be able to put down her answer as 'writer'. Then it asked what Carol did for relaxation. After chewing her pen for a moment Carol put down the truth—'writing'. The third question asked: 'What are your hobbies?' Well, not wanting to look obsessed or, worse still, boring, she crossed the fingers on her free hand and answered 'swimming and tennis'. But, given that the chlorine in the pool does terrible things to her highlights, and the closest she's got to a tennis racket in the last couple of years is watching the Australian Open, I'm sure you can guess the real answer!

Books by Carol Marinelli

Mills & Boon® Medical Romance™

London's Most Desirable Docs

Unwrapping Her Italian Doc
Playing the Playboy's Sweetheart

Bayside Hospital Heartbreakers!

Tempted by Dr Morales
The Accidental Romeo

Secrets of a Career Girl
Dr Dark and Far Too Delicious
NYC Angels: Redeeming the Playboy
200 Harley Street: Surgeon in a Tux
Baby Twins to Bind Them
Just One Night?

**Visit the author profile page at
millsandboon.co.uk for more titles**

**Praise for
Carol Marinelli**

'A compelling, sensual, sexy, emotionally packed,
drama-filled read that will leave you begging for more!'
—*Contemporary Romance Reviews* on
NYC Angels: Redeeming the Playboy

PROLOGUE

THIS WASN'T HOW July was supposed to be.

'Hey, Cat!'

Catriona Hayes stood as her friend came out of her office but she was unable to return Gemma's smile. 'I've just got to go up to Maternity to see a patient and then we can...' Gemma didn't finish her sentence. Now she was closer she could see that her friend was barely holding it together—Cat's green eyes were brimming with tears, her long curly black hair looked as if it had been whipped up by the wind and she was a touch breathless, as if she'd been running. It quickly became clear to Gemma that Cat was not here at the London Royal for their shopping date.

She wasn't.

Cat had walked out of her antenatal appointment at the hospital where she worked and, like a homing beacon, had taken the underground to the Royal, where Gemma was an obstetrics registrar. She had sat in panicked silence on the tube and, despite being twenty weeks pregnant and wearing a flimsy wraparound dress and heels, she had been one of those people running up the escalator rather than standing and letting it take them to the top.

'You're not here for our shopping date, are you?' Gemma checked, and Cat vaguely recalled a date that they had made a couple of weeks ago. They were both supposed to finish at four today and the plan had been to hit the shops, given that Cat would know by now if she was having a boy or girl.

They had had it all planned—they were going to head off for a late afternoon tea and Cat would reveal the news about the sex of her baby. Then they would shop for baby things in the appropriate colours and choose shoes for Cat and Mike's wedding, which was just over three weeks away.

That was how it was supposed to be.

This was how it was.

'You know how we discussed keeping things separate?' Cat felt as if her voice didn't belong to her as she spoke to her closest friend. 'Can I change my mind about that?'

And, because she and Gemma had been friends since way back in medical school, she didn't have to explain what she meant.

'Of course you can,' Gemma said, battling a feeling of dread. 'Let's go into my office.'

When Cat had found out that she was pregnant she had discussed with her family doctor, and also her fiancé, the potential pitfalls of having your closest friend as your obstetrician.

Against her own gut instinct, an esteemed colleague of Mike's was now overseeing her pregnancy.

She had walked out on both of them today.

Now Cat walked into her friend's office on shaky legs and, for the first time as Gemma's patient, took a seat, wondering how best to explain what had been going on in her life. The past two weeks she had dodged speaking with Gemma as best she could.

Gemma poured her a glass of water and Cat took a long drink as her friend waited patiently. Finally she caught her breath enough to speak.

'I had an ultrasound a couple of weeks ago,' she started. 'There were some problems… I know I could have spoken to you but Mike wanted to wait for all the test results to be in before we told anyone. *If* we told anyone…' Tears were now falling thick and fast but she had run out of sobs and so was able to continue. 'The results are not good, Gemma. They're not good at all. I had an amnio and the baby has Edwards syndrome…' Cat elaborated further. 'Full-form Edwards syndrome.' She looked at her friend and saw Gemma's small swallow as she took in the diagnosis.

'What does Mike say?'

Not only had Cat found out her baby was terribly sick, but also in these past two weeks her relationship had crumbled.

'Mike says that it's not part of the plan… Well, he didn't have the guts to say it like that. He said that as a paediatrician he knows better than most what the baby would be up against and what we'd be up against—the anomalies are very severe. There really isn't much hope that it will survive the birth and if it does it's likely to live only for a few hours.' Her voice was starting to rise. 'He says that it's not our fault, that we've every chance of a healthy baby and so we should put it behind us and try again…' Cat's eyes flashed in anger. 'He's a paediatrician, for God's sake, and he wants me to have a late abortion…'

'What do you want, Cat?' her friend gently broke in. 'Do you even know what you want?'

'A healthy baby.'

Gemma just looked.

'And that's not going to happen,' Cat said.

Finally she had accepted it.

She sat there in silence. It was the first glimpse of peace she had had in two weeks. Since the first ultrasound, at Mike's strong suggestion, they had kept the findings to themselves and so she had been holding it all in—somehow working as an emergency registrar, as well as carrying on with their wedding plans and doing her best to avoid catching up with Gemma.

At first Cat had woken in tears and dread for her baby each morning. Today, though, she had woken in anger and, looking at the back of her fiancé's head and seeing him deeply asleep, instead of waiting for him to wake up, she had dug him in the ribs.

'What's wrong?' Mike had turned to her rage and she had told him they were through. That even if, by some miracle, the amnio came back as normal today, there was nothing left of them.

The amnio hadn't come back as normal.

Cat had known that it wouldn't; she'd seen the ultrasound and nothing could magic the problems away.

It had been confirmation, that was all.

Now Gemma gave her the gift of a pause and Cat sat, feeling the little kicks of her baby inside her as well as the rapid thud of her own heart. Finally both settled down as she came to the decision she had been reaching towards since the news had first hit.

'I understand that it's different for everyone. Maybe

if I'd found out sooner I'd have had a termination.' She truly didn't know what she might have done then; she could only deal with her feelings now. 'But I'm twenty weeks pregnant. I know it's a boy and I can feel him move. He's moving right now.' She put a hand on her stomach and felt him, in there and alive and safe. 'Mike keeps saying it would be kinder but I'm starting to wonder, kinder for whom?'

Gemma was patient and Cat waited as she rang through to the hospital where Cat was being seen and all the results were transferred.

Gemma went through them carefully.

And she didn't leave it there; instead, she made a phone call to a colleague and Cat underwent yet another ultrasound.

Her baby was imperfect, from his too-little head to his tiny curved feet, but all Cat could see was her son. Gently Gemma told her that the condition was very severe, as she'd been told, and she concurred that if the baby survived birth he would live only for a little while.

'I want whatever time I have with him,' Cat said.

'I'll be there with you,' Gemma said. 'Mike might—'

'I'm not discussing it further with Mike,' Cat said. 'I'll tell him what I've decided and it's up to him what he does, but as a couple we're finished.'

'You don't have to make any rash decisions about your relationship. It's a lot for any couple to take in...'

'We're not a couple any more,' Cat said. 'I told him that this morning—as soon as things started to go wrong with the pregnancy, even before things went wrong, I felt as if I didn't have a voice. Well, I do and I'm having my baby.'

* * *

It was a long month, a difficult month but a very precious one.

Cat cancelled the wedding while knowing soon she would be arranging a funeral but she pushed that thought aside as best she could.

Her parents were little help. Her mother agreed with Mike; her father just disappeared into his study if ever Cat came round. But she had Greg, her brother, who cleared out all her things from Mike's house.

He didn't hit him, much to Cat's relief.

Almost, though!

And, of course, she had Gemma.

At the end of July and at twenty-five weeks gestation Cat went into spontaneous labour and Gemma delivered her a little son. Thomas Gregory Hayes. Thomas because she loved the name. Gregory, after her brother. Hayes because it was her surname.

Cat would treasure every minute of the two precious days and one night that Thomas lived.

Most of them.

His severe cleft palate meant she couldn't feed him, though she ached to. She would never get out of her mind the image of her mother's grimace when she'd seen her grandson and his deformities—Cat had asked her to leave.

For two days she had closed the door to her room on the maternity ward and had let only love enter.

Her brother, Gemma and her new boyfriend, Nigel, a couple of other lifelong friends, along with the medical staff helped her care for him—and all played their part.

When Cat had no choice but to sleep, Greg, Gemma

or Nigel nursed him and Thomas wasn't once, apart from having his nappy changed, put down.

His whole life Thomas knew only love.

After the funeral, when her parents and some other family members had tried to tell her that maybe Thomas's passing was a blessing, it was Gemma who held Cat's hand as she bit back a caustic response.

Instead of doing as suggested and putting it all behind her and attempting a new normal, Cat took all her maternity leave and hid for a while to grieve. But as her return-to-work date approached she felt less and less inclined to go back, especially as Mike still worked there.

She applied for a position in the accident and emergency department at the London Royal, where her baby had been born and where Gemma worked.

Four months to the day that she'd lost her son Cat stepped back out into the world... Only, she wasn't the same.

Instead, she was a far tougher version of her old self.

CHAPTER ONE

Seven years later

'YOU'RE FAR TOO cynical about men, Cat.'

'I don't think that I am,' Cat answered, 'though admittedly I'd love to be proven wrong. But, no, I'm taking a full year off men.'

Cat was busy packing. Just out of the shower she was wearing a dressing gown and her long, curly black hair was wrapped in a towel. As she pulled clothes out of her wardrobe she chatted to her close friend Gemma, who was lying on Cat's bed and answering emails on her phone.

They were two very busy women but they usually managed to catch up a couple of times a week, whether at the hospital canteen, a coffee shop or wine bar, or just a quick drop-in at the other's home.

This evening Cat was heading to Barcelona for an international emergency medicine conference, where she was going to be giving a talk the following morning. She had got off early from her shift at the hospital to pack and Gemma had popped around to finalise a few details for the following weekend. Gemma and

Nigel's twin boys, Rory and Marcus, were being christened and Cat was to be godmother to Rory.

They were used to catching up on the run. Any plans
they made were all too often cancelled at the last minute thanks to Cat's position as an accident and emergency consultant and Gemma juggling being a mother
to two eighteen-month-old boys as well as a full-time
obstetrician.

Their lives were similar in many ways and very different in others.

'So you and Rick have definitely broken up?' Gemma
checked that Cat's latest relationship was really over.

'He's been gone a month, so I'd say so!'

'You're not even going to think about it?'

'Why would I consider moving to Yorkshire when
I'm happy here?'

'Because that's what couples do.'

'Oh, so if Nigel suddenly decided that he wanted
to move to...' Cat thought for a moment and then remembered that Nigel was taking French lessons. 'If
he wanted to move to France, you're telling me that
you'd go?'

'Not without consideration,' Gemma said. 'Given that
I'm the breadwinner there would have to be a good reason, but if Nigel really wanted to, then, of course, I'd give
it some thought. Relationships are about compromise.'

'And it's always the woman who has to be the one
to compromise,' Cat said, but Gemma shook her head.

'I don't agree.'

'You've never played the dating game in your thirties.'

'Yes, I have—Nigel and I only married last year.'

'Ah, but the two of you had been going out for ever
before then. It's different at our age, Gemma. Men

might say that they don't mind independent working women and, of course, they don't—just as long as you're home before them and have the dinner on.'

'Rubbish!' Gemma responded from her happily married vantage point. 'Look at Nigel—I work, he gave up teaching and stays home and looks after the children, and the house and me...'

'Yes.' Cat smiled. 'Well, you and Nigel are a very rare exception to my well-proven theory.'

But Gemma suddenly had other things on her mind when she saw what Cat was about to add to her case. 'Please don't take them,' Gemma said, referring to Cat's running shoes. 'They're ugly.'

'They're practical,' Cat said. 'And they are also very comfortable. I'm hoping to squeeze in a little bit of sightseeing on Sunday afternoon once the conference wraps up. There's a modern art museum, hopefully I'll get some inspiration for this room...'

She looked around at the disgusting beige walls and beige carpet and beige curtains and wished she knew what she wanted to do with the room.

Gemma got off the bed and went to Cat's wardrobe and took out some espadrilles.

'Take these instead.'

'For walking?'

'Yes, Cat, for walking, not striding...' She peered into her friend's luggage. 'Talk about shades of grey—that's the saddest case I've ever seen. You're going to Spain!'

'I'm going to Spain for two nights to catch the end of a conference. I'm not going on a holiday. I shan't even see the beach,' Cat pointed out. 'I wish that I *was* flying off for a holiday,' she said, and then sat on the bed. 'I hate July so much.'

'I know you do.'

It had been seven years since Thomas had died.

She didn't lug her grief around all the time but on days like today it hurt. Gemma smiled as her friend went into her bedside drawer and took out his photo. Cat kept it there; it was close enough that she could look at it any time and removed enough not to move her to tears. The drawer also meant she didn't have to explain the most vital piece of her past to any lovers until she was ready to.

She simply found it too painful.

'Rick asked how likely I was to have another one like him,' Cat admitted. It was what had really caused the end of her latest relationship. 'I told him about Thomas and then I showed him his photo…'

'He's not a doctor, Cat,' Gemma said. 'It's a normal question to ask. It's one you've asked.'

'I know that. It was more the way…' She was so hypersensitive to people's reactions when they saw her son but she smiled when Gemma spoke on.

'I loved how he smiled if you touched his little feet,' Gemma said, and her words confirmed to Cat that she was very blessed to have such a wonderful friend. 'He's so beautiful.'

He was.

Not to others perhaps but they had both seen his lovely eyes and felt his little fingers curve around theirs and they had felt his soft skin and heard his little cries.

And this was the hard part.

It was late July and she'd be away on *those* days.

The day of Thomas's birth and also the day that he had died.

'Do I take his photo with me?' Cat asked, and Gemma thought for a moment.

'I don't think you need his photo to remember him,' she said.

'But I feel guilty leaving him in the drawer.'

'Leave him with me, then,' Gemma said. 'I'll have a long gaze.'

Yes, she had the very best friend in the world, Cat thought as she handed over her most precious possession, and because she was going to start crying Cat changed the subject. 'Hey, did you have any luck tracking down that dress for the christening?'

'Nope.'

Gemma shook her head as she put the photo in her bag. 'I knew that I should have just bought it when I saw it. It was perfect.'

'It was very nice, but…' Cat didn't continue. A white broderie anglaise halter-neck with a flowing skirt was a bit over the top for Cat's tastes but, then, that was Gemma.

And this was her.

She pulled on some white linen pants and a coloured top *and* added the espadrilles.

'Am I girlie enough for you now?'

'You look great.' Gemma laughed. 'It's once you get there that worries me. With those clothes you'll just blend in with all the others…'

'Which is exactly my intention,' Cat said. 'I have to go soon.'

'But your flight's not till nine.'

'I know but I've booked in to get my hair blow-dried on the way.'

Her long black curls would be straightened, just as

they were twice a week. Cat always washed it herself before she went to the hairdresser's, though.

It saved time.

They headed downstairs, chatting as Cat did a few last-minute things. 'You're speaking in the morning?' Gemma checked.

'At nine.' Cat nodded. 'I'd have loved to have flown last night but I couldn't get away. Hamish isn't back till tomorrow and Andrew is covering me this weekend. Same old. It would have been nice to stay on for a bit and spend a few days in Barcelona…'

'Are you ever going to take some time off?'

'I'm off in October for three weeks.' Cat smiled. 'My exams will be done and I'm going to celebrate by decorating my bedroom. I can't wait to turn it into something that doesn't make me want to sleep downstairs on the sofa.'

'You've done an amazing job with the house.'

Last year, after a year of looking, Cat had bought a small two-bedroom home in a leafy London suburb. It was a twenty-minute drive to work at night, which meant, if Cat was on call, that she had to stay at the hospital. Yes, perhaps she could have bought somewhere just a little bit closer but the drive did mean that when she left the hospital, she really left the building.

Here, she could pull on tatty shorts and a T-shirt and get on with her second love—knocking down walls, plastering and painting. The house had been a real renovator's delight and Cat had delighted in renovating it.

The ghastly purple carpet had been ripped up to expose floorboards that, once sanded and oiled, brought a warmth to the house. A false wall in the lounge had been removed to reveal a fireplace and the once-purple-themed bathroom was now tiled white with dark wood fittings and had a gorgeous claw-foot bath.

'Will you sell it once you've decorated the bedroom?'

'I really don't know,' Cat admitted, tipping milk down the sink. 'Initially that was the plan, but now I love the place and want to simply enjoy it, but…'

'But?'

'I've really enjoyed doing it up bit by bit. I'm going to miss that.'

'After your bedroom you've still got the garden to make over.'

'Oh, no!' Cat shook her head. 'I'll get someone in to do that.'

As they headed out, Cat locked up and Gemma looked at the small front garden.

'It's the size of a stamp,' Gemma pointed out. There was just a rickety path and two neglected flower beds, and the back garden, Gemma knew, was a small strip of grass and an old wooden shed. 'You could have it sorted in a few days…'

'Nope!' Cat smiled. 'I have black thumbs.'

They said goodbye on the street.

'We'll catch up properly soon,' Cat promised. Both women knew that they wouldn't get much of a chance to gossip at the christening. 'I'll come over to yours after the conference. I haven't seen the twins for ages. I'll bring them a stuffed donkey each back from Spain.'

'Please, don't!' Gemma winced and glanced at her phone to check the time. 'Ooh, I might make it home in time to give them their bath before bed. Nigel's cooking a romantic dinner for the two of us tonight…'

'Lovely.'

'Enjoy Spain,' Gemma called. 'You might find yourself some sexy Spanish flamenco dancer or matador...'

'At an emergency medicine conference?' Cat laughed. 'I don't think there's much chance of that.'

'Well, a gorgeous waiter, with come-to-bed eyes and—'

'Oh, please!'

'Why not?' Gemma winked. 'If you can't manage a love life, then pencil a few flings into that overcrowded diary of yours.'

'There's another conference in Spain the following week that *you* might want to consider attending,' Cat said in a dry voice. 'Sexual health. You, as an obstetrician, better than anyone must know the perils of casual sex.'

'Of course I do, but sex *is* healthy.' Gemma grinned and then she looked at Cat. She wanted to pick up an imaginary sledgehammer of her own and knock down the wall that had gone up around her friend since her baby's death.

'Do you know what's brilliant about a one-night stand, Cat?'

'Gemma...' Cat shook her head. She really didn't have time to stand and chat but her friend persisted.

Gemma loved to talk about sex! 'He doesn't have to be perfect, you don't have to worry how you might slot into each other's lives and whether he leaves the toilet seat up or is going to support you in your career and all that stuff, because you're not looking for a potential Mr Right. He can be Mr Wrong, Mr Bad, Mr Whatever-It-Is-You-Fancy. God, but I miss one-night stands.'

'Does Nigel know your theory?'

'Of course he doesn't.' Gemma grinned. 'Nigel still thinks he was my second...' They both laughed for a moment but then Gemma stood firm. 'It's time for you to have some fun, Cat. Doctor's orders—you're to buy some condoms at the airport.'

Cat laughed and waved and got into her car and headed for the hairdresser's.

She adored Gemma.

And Nigel.

But…

What she hadn't said to her very good friend was that, as much as it might work for Gemma, she really didn't want a Nigel of her own. She didn't want someone asking what was for dinner every night, but nor did she want to be the one coming in after work and doing the 'Hi, honey, I'm home' thing.

Still, there wasn't time to dwell on it all.

She parked her car in her usual spot behind the church and grabbed her bag and walked quickly to the hairdresser's. She pushed on the door but it didn't open and she frowned and then she saw the 'Closed' sign.

'Don't do this to me, Glynn…'

He never forgot her appointments and Cat had been very specific about the time for today when she had seen him on Monday. Glynn knew that she had a plane to catch and that she would be pushed for time.

'Breathe,' Cat mumbled as she accepted that no amount of rattling the door was going to make Glynn suddenly appear.

It's a hair appointment, that's all, she told herself. There would be a hairdresser at the hotel. Only, her presentation was at nine in the morning and she'd wanted to have a leisurely breakfast in her room and calm herself down before that.

And it was Thomas's birthday tomorrow.

She was not going to cry over a missed hair appointment.

Cat wasn't crying over that as she drove to the airport. Instead, she was wishing the boot was full of presents and wrapping paper and that she was dashing to pick up a birthday cake...

Why was it still so hard?

So, as she could not get her thick curly hair smoothed into long, glossy and straight, she bought some hair serum at the airport, then checked in her luggage and headed through with ages to spare.

She went to the loos and sorted her hair as best she could, deciding she would straighten it tonight and again in the morning, but for now she tied it back and headed out.

She took a seat and read through her talk on her tablet. It was about palliative care and its place in the emergency department and, really, she knew it back to front and inside out. She had done hours of research and all her meticulous notes and patient studies now came down to one talk.

And then what?

Exams.

And then?

Cat blew out a breath.

Her career was a little like her house renovation.

The day she'd moved in Cat had stared at the purple carpet and the purple tiles that would take for ever to get off. It had seemed unlikely, near impossible, that she would ever get there and yet here she was, just a bedroom and a garden away from completion.

She had, through high school, always wanted to be a surgeon yet as a medical student she had stepped into the emergency department and had been quickly ushered into Resus to observe the treatment of a patient who had just come in.

A cyclist had lain there unconscious with a massive head injury. Cat had watched in silent awe as the staff had brought his dire condition under control. His heart, which hadn't been beating, had been restarted. His airway had been secured and the seizures that had then started to rack his body had been halted with drugs.

She had been sure at first that he would die and yet he had made it to Theatre and then on to Intensive Care.

She had followed him up and found out a week later that he had been transferred to a ward. She had gone in to see him, expecting what, she hadn't known. Certainly not a young man sitting up in bed, laughing and talking with his girlfriend, who was sitting by his side.

He should be dead, Cat had thought, though, of course, she didn't say that. Instead, she'd chatted to him for a few moments, unable to truly comprehend that here he was, not just alive but laughing and living.

Emergency medicine had become her passion right there and then. Yes, at twenty years old she had known she was a long way off being as skilled as the staff who had attended the cyclist that day.

Slowly she had got there, though.

And now here she was, coming to the top of her game.

So why the restlessness?

Cat glanced up at the board and rolled her eyes when she saw that her flight was delayed, and decided to wander around the shops.

Oh, there was Gemma's dress!

She was sure that it was, though looking at the price tag, not quite sure enough to buy it without checking, so she took a photo and fired a quick text to her friend.

Is this it?

It was, and Gemma promised to love her for ever and forgive any stuffed donkeys she might bring home for the twins if Cat would buy it for her.

She bought some duty-free perfume too, as well as her favourite lip gloss and…no—no condoms.

Finally the plane was boarding and Cat, along with her purchases, was on her way.

She didn't read through her talk again. She dozed most of the way, trying to drown out the sound of over-excited children and their parents. As they disembarked she almost forgot the dress but luckily she grabbed it at the last minute.

Very luckily, as it turned out.

Having spent hours watching an empty baggage carousel, seeing the shutters go down on all the airport shops and filling in numerous forms, she was doing her level best to hold it together as she climbed out of the taxi and walked into the hotel. It was close to midnight.

Her luggage was lost, her hair was a joke.

And tomorrow, at nine, she had to deliver the most important presentation of her life.

CHAPTER TWO

CAT WOKE BEFORE her breakfast was delivered and lay there.

She remembered a day seven years ago and wished, how she wished, that there was a seven-year-old waiting to open his birthday presents and to sing 'Happy Birthday' to.

It was a hard picture to paint and each year it got harder.

Was Mike in this happy family picture and did Thomas have brothers and sisters now?

No, she didn't miss Mike and the perfect world they had been building. She missed, on Thomas's behalf, all that he had been denied.

She couldn't afford to cry, especially given the fact she had no make-up with her and so she headed to the bathroom to set to work with the little she had.

With her heavy-duty hair straighteners neatly packed in her lost luggage, she was very grateful for the hair serum she had bought and applied an awful lot in an attempt to tame her long, wild curly hair.

When her breakfast was delivered she walked out onto the balcony and tried to calm herself with the spectacular view of the Mediterranean. It was just after seven but already the air was warm. The coffee was hot and strong and Cat tried to focus on her speech. *It will be fine,* she told herself, refusing to fall apart because she didn't have the perfect, *perfect* pale grey suit and the pale ballet pumps in the softest buttery leather to wear.

They were here to hear her words, Cat reminded herself.

Yet she couldn't quite convince herself that it didn't matter what she wore or how she looked.

Neutral.

That was how she always tried to appear.

There was nothing neutral about her today, she thought as she slipped on Gemma's dress.

Her rather ample bust was accentuated by the lace, the halter-neck showed far too much of her brown back—the tan was from painting the window frames on her last lot of days off, rather than lying on the beach. Her hair she tied back with the little white band that came with the shower cap in the bathroom and then she covered it with a thick strand of black hair.

A squirt of duty-free perfume, a slick of lip gloss and she would simply have to do.

Yet, she thought, having tied up her espadrilles, as she stood and looked in the mirror, while never in a million years would she have chosen this outfit for anything related to work, she liked how it looked. She wouldn't even have chosen it for anything out of work either. Generally she was in shorts or jeans when sorting out the renovations. Yes, she liked how she looked today. It reminded her of how she had looked before she'd had...

Cat halted herself right there.

She simply could not afford the luxury of breaking down.

Tonight, Cat told herself. Tonight she would order room service and a bottle of wine and reminisce.

Today she had to get on.

She had one last flick through her notes and then she headed out to register for the conference and also to check that everything was in place for her talk.

She was just putting her swipe card in her bag when the elevator doors opened and she looked up to an empty lift, bar one occupant.

Bar One was tall and unshaven with grey eyes and his dark hair was a touch too long yet he looked effortlessly smart in dark pants and a white shirt. All this she noted as she stood there and briefly wondered if she should simply let this lift go.

For some bizarre reason that seemed far easier than stepping in.

'Buenos días,' Bar One said, and then frowned at her indecision as to whether or not to enter.

'Buenos días,' Cat replied, gave him a brisk smile and stepped in. The floor number for the function rooms had already been pressed and as she glanced to the side and down, anywhere other than his eyes, she noted he too was an owner of the softest buttery leather shoes.

His luggage clearly hadn't been lost.

And neither was he wearing socks.

Three, Cat thought as his cologne met her nostrils and she found herself doing a very quick audit as to the number of garments that would remain on his lovely body once he'd kicked off those shoes.

Talk about thinking like a man!

She blamed Gemma, of course. It was her fault for

putting such ideas in her head, Cat decided as the lift opened at the next floor and unfortunately no one got in.

He said something else in Spanish and Cat shook her head. 'Actually, *buenos días* is as far as my Spanish goes.'

'Oh,' he said. 'I thought you were a local.'

His accent was English and he had just delivered a compliment indeed, because the locals, Cat had worked out during her prolonged time at the airport last night, were a pretty stunning lot.

'Nope.' She shook her head.

The lift doors opened and he wished her a good day as he went to step out.

'And you,' she offered.

'Sadly not,' he replied, and nodded to the gathering crowd outside the elevators. 'I'm working.'

'So am I,' she said, and he stood there a little taken aback as he let her out first.

Oh!

Dominic had thought she was on her way to some… Well, he'd had no idea really where she might have been on her way to but talk about a sight for sore eyes.

She had a very, very nice back, he decided as he followed her over to the registration desk, where there was a small line-up.

A very tense back, he noted as she reached into her bag and pulled out her phone.

'I'm Dominic…'

Cat had just had a text from the airline to say her luggage had been found. At Gatwick! It *should* be with her later this afternoon and could she confirm that she was still at the same hotel. She barely turned around as she fired back a text and told him her name. 'Cat.'

'Short for?'

She really didn't have time for small talk and she knew, just knew, because her back was scalding from his eyes, that it was more than small talk he was offering. 'I'm actually a bit busy at the moment...'

'Well, that's some name—no wonder you have to shorten it.'

Her fingers hesitated over the text she was typing and she gave a small, presumably unseen smile.

Dominic, even if he couldn't see her mouth, knew from behind that she'd smiled.

He watched as that rigid spinal column very briefly relaxed a notch and those tense shoulders dropped a fraction.

Still, he left things there. He certainly wasn't going to pursue a conversation that had been so swiftly shut down.

Instead, he looked at the brochure with only mild interest. He loathed this type of thing. He'd only put his hand up because he'd needed the update hours and because his parents and sister lived nearby—it would be a good chance to catch up. As well as that, he was seriously considering moving here.

He kept himself up to date and found these presentations pointless, or rather bullet-pointed—most speakers had everything on slides and it was rather like being read a bedtime story out loud. At thirty-two years of age, he would rather read for himself.

'Dominic!'

He glanced over at the sound of his name and gave a smile when he saw that it was someone he had studied with in London.

'How are you, Hugh?'

Cat stood there, trying not to notice the delicious depth to his voice. Not that he spoke much; it was his friend who did most of the talking.

She registered and was told that one of the organisers would be with her shortly to take her to where her talk was being held.

'This way, Dr Hayes...'

Dominic stopped in mid-sentence as Cat was led away. She must be speaking, he realised, and, quite shamelessly, he glanced through the list of speakers and found out her name for himself.

Catriona Hayes.

And then he saw the topic of her talk.

Palliative Care and its Place in the Emergency Department.

Absolutely *not* what he needed.

So, instead of hearing her speak, he took himself off to listen to a disaster management panel but his mind wasn't really there. Half an hour later he slipped out unnoticed and slipped into where she was talking.

She noticed him come in.

There was a tiny pause in her talk as she glanced at the opening door and saw *him* enter.

He didn't take a seat but leant against the back wall with arms folded. There was a small falter in her flawless talk as he took his place but then she continued where she'd left off.

'Of course, it's great for the patient when they receive a terminal diagnosis to take that break, that trek, that overseas trip. It can just be a touch inconvenient for us when they present, minus notes, diagnosis, information and family. And so, because that's what we do, we leap in and do our best to save them.' She looked out at the room. 'Of course, it's not so great for the patient either when they come around to our smiling faces… It's hard on the staff when a four-year-old presents on Christmas Eve. It's our instinct to do all that we can. There isn't always time to speak at length with the family when they come rushing in with their child but listen we must…'

It wasn't like a bedtime story with everything spelt out. Yes, there were bullet points, but they were only brief outlines and, for Dominic, a lot of her words felt like bullets as she filled in the gaps.

Brusque was her delivery as she covered things such as legalities, next of kin, patient rights. For good measure, staff, relative and patient guilt was thrown in too.

He listened, he felt, yet his face never moved a muscle.

As she finished, he left the room and went off to lunch but, even if it smelt fantastic, food didn't appeal and instead he took some water and went out onto a large balcony.

Unlike others who had been at her talk Dominic didn't go up and congratulate her. Neither did he tell her that her talk had touched a nerve.

He could have walked over and said how his wife had got up in the night and wandered off. He could have said how angry she had been to wake up two days later in ICU and that he could still see the reproach in her eyes, as if Dominic had somehow failed her because she'd lived.

No, he didn't need or want *that* look from Cat and he was tired, so tired of women who gave out sympathy and understanding.

He'd prefer something lighter.

Or darker, perhaps! Hopefully, Dominic thought, heading back in, so too would she.

CHAPTER THREE

IT WOULD BE an absolute lie to say the attraction hadn't been as instant as it was mutual.

All through the lunch break there was a knot high in Cat's stomach and tension in her muscles and she knew that she was bracing herself for him to come over.

Except he didn't.

Ouch!

She wasn't sure if she even wanted him to.

There was an arrogance to him, not that she couldn't handle arrogant men; she'd dealt with more than her share of them.

No, it was something else about Dominic that had her seriously rattled—the presumption of sex.

From the briefest conversation she had gleaned that much. From the roam of his eyes on the bare skin of her back, from the sullen, one-sided conversation with his friend that had told her his mind was on her.

From the corner of her eye she watched as he came in from the balcony and then went over and chatted to a group.

She was incredibly aware of his presence and it had been a long time since she had felt anything close to that.

Not that it mattered.

She was being ignored.

Funny, but she knew that it was deliberate and what was stranger still it made her smile. 'Excellent talk...' A middle-aged blond man came over and introduced himself. 'Gordon.' He smiled.

'Cat.'

It was a very long thirty minutes.

Gordon simply didn't let up and Cat couldn't really make her excuses and leave because he was talking about his wife who had died and the total hash that had been made in the emergency department.

It was a busman's holiday for Cat as she lined up for the lovely buffet lunch and Gordon followed her with his plate.

'Two hours, we waited, Cat,' he said, and she glanced up and met those gorgeous grey eyes and saw that Dominic was now unashamedly watching her.

Rescue me, her green ones said, but he looked away.

'And then...' Gordon continued to tell her about his wife's IV coming out and the drugs that didn't go in. Yes, it was a sad story, but it was a story she dealt with every day and it was her lunch break.

'Paella, please.' Cat held out her plate to the waiter but he shook his head.

'We're waiting for some more...'

Cat chose some odd noodle salad, just to get away, but Gordon chose the same and he was off again. He sat next to her at a high table and droned on and on.

She met Dominic's eyes again and this time he smiled.

You missed your chance, his eyes said.

I've changed my mind, was her silent plea.

Well, you're too late!

He yawned and pulled out his pamphlet and with a very small smirk walked off.

What a bastard.

Cat laughed and then turned to Gordon's confused expression.

'I said, then she died…'

'Sorry, I thought you said then she…' Cat let out a breath. 'What a terrible time you had.'

She just didn't need to hear about it today of all days.

She didn't see Dominic again all afternoon, not that it mattered by then. At 5:00 p.m. when she got back to her room to find that her luggage still hadn't arrived, it wasn't the Spanish-speaking English doctor who was on her mind.

It was Thomas.

She didn't want to go down for dinner in an hour and be sociable.

Room service seemed a far better idea.

A huge plate of paella.

A bottle of wine.

She wished she'd brought his photo.

But there had been too many sad birthdays and, suddenly realising that she had a very small window if she didn't want to spend tomorrow dressed in Gemma's dress or linen pants that were more suitable for travel, she headed out.

She found herself in a large department store, explaining to an orange woman that, apart from a lipstick, she had no make-up with her.

'My luggage was lost,' she said.

The woman was so horrified on her behalf that Cat actually smiled. 'It's fine…'

It was.

So much so that instead of buying loads of make-up and then heading upstairs to the *ropa de señora* section to purchase a chic Spanish outfit Cat wandered out and found herself drawn to a busy market. There were gorgeous dresses blowing in the late-afternoon breeze and they were nothing like what she usually wore.

If she walked into work dressed as she was today, it would draw comment. Here, apart from a couple of vaguely familiar faces from conferences of long ago, no one knew her.

It was incredibly freeing—she could be whoever she chose to be.

Cat took her time with her purchases. She chose a loose long dress in lilac and shorts that were very short, along with a top and a stringy-looking bikini. And, she decided, instead of the museum on Sunday afternoon she was going to the beach.

She liked Barcelona.

Far more than she had expected to.

It was cosmopolitan, busy yet friendly, colourful and hot.

Walking back into the hotel, she was about to take her purchases up and get changed and, instead of hiding in her room, perhaps head out for dinner by herself when she saw him.

Dominic.

'I was wondering where you were,' he said by way of greeting, and Cat liked it that he was direct.

'I went shopping…' She was about to explain that her luggage was lost but then decided she didn't have to explain anything.

'Cat!' a voice boomed, and she turned and saw that

Gordon was bearing down on her. 'There's a group of us heading to the hotel restaurant. Why don't you join us?'

'Oh, I'd love to but I can't,' Cat said. 'I'm expecting a call. A conference call. I—'

'Maybe after?' Gordon checked.

'I'll try.'

Gordon smiled over to Dominic. 'Do you have plans or would you like to join us?'

Dominic dealt with things far more effortlessly than Cat. 'I've already got plans, but thank you for asking.'

As the group walked off they were left standing.

'Liar,' Dominic said. 'You don't have a conference call you have to get to.'

'Was it obvious?' she groaned.

'To me it was.' Dominic nodded. 'Liars always have a need to elaborate. You'd know that, working in Emergency.'

'I know,' she said. 'So would Gordon.'

'Is he a friend?'

Cat shook her head.

'A colleague?'

'No.'

'So why not just say no if it's something that you don't want to do?'

'I know that I should. I just feel bad...'

'Well, don't—he's far too busy banging on about his late wife to notice what others are feeling.'

She felt her nostrils tighten. 'That was mean.'

'No,' Dominic refuted. 'He tried to run the whole sorry story by me yesterday. What's mean is buttonholing a relative stranger and completely ruining their lunch.'

He shrugged.

He was dismissive.

She didn't like that and she was about to head off when he halted her in her tracks.

'Do you want dinner away from the hotel?'

'I've got a conference call to make,' she said, and gave him a tight smile.

'Sure?' he said.

Usually, yes.

She didn't like his dismissal of Gordon but, apart from that, he was, well, deliciously overwhelming.

Gemma's words were ringing in her ears. He didn't have to be perfect, he didn't have to be anything other than…

God, but she fancied him.

She could have left it there, just walked off and it would have been over. There were no games, no pretence, just his question, which she now answered truthfully. 'Dinner away from the hotel sounds great,' she said. 'I'll just…' She held up her bags and was about to suggest that she take them up and meet him back here in…half an hour, or however long it took to get showered and dressed.

But by then she'd have changed her mind, she knew.

Half an hour from now she'd be calling Reception to pass on a message to him.

Or she could just go with how she felt now.

'I'll just ask Reception if they can take my bags up.'

The streets were noisy and he navigated them easily and took her to a place that Cat would never have found had she explored on her own—a few streets along from the strip the hotel was on. They walked down a stone stairwell and to an *asado* restaurant that was noisy and smoky, even with the open area out the back.

'So, are you pleased your talk is over?' he asked when they were tucked away at a table.

'Very,' Cat said. 'I can relax now.'

And relax she did, admitting she had no clue about Spanish wine and letting him choose.

'Are you staying till Monday?' he asked, and she shook her head.

'No, I fly out tomorrow evening—I'm back at work on Monday. I wish…'

'Wish what?'

'Well, I was really only thinking of my talk when I booked the flights. I wasn't actually expecting to like Barcelona so much. I should have tagged on a couple of days' annual leave and done a bit of exploring.'

'You always could.'

It sounded very tempting but it was a little too late for that now. 'We're pretty short on staff at the moment. My colleague Andrew is going on leave and Hamish, he's the other consultant…' She rolled her eyes. 'I'm sure you know how it is.'

'Remind me,' he said.

'Remind you?' she checked. 'Where do you work?'

'Scotland.'

She waited for him to elaborate, which he did but it was vague rather than specific. 'I work a little bit here and a longer bit there,' Dominic said, and Cat then felt the scrutiny of his gaze and the message behind his words as he spoke on. 'I don't like to be tied to one place.' And then he elaborated properly. 'Or one person.'

Well, that certainly told her.

In part, Cat was tempted to simply get up and leave. It wasn't a meal, they both knew that. This wasn't two like-minded colleagues sharing a dinner after a busy day at a conference.

This was exactly what the dear Dr Gemma had ordered.

Cat was old enough to know it.

Their knees were nudging and suddenly her lips felt too big for her face without the resting place of his mouth.

She felt his eyes glance down as she reached for her drink and from the sudden weight in her breasts she knew where his glance had been. Only, it wasn't sleazy. Or, if it was, it came from both of them because she'd been doing the same to his bum a little earlier as he'd walked down the stairs.

No, this wasn't just dinner.

'Do you have a problem with that?' he said, and she blinked as she tried to remember the conversation. Oh, yes, the not-tied-to-one-person thing, he was asking if she had a problem with that.

Did she?

Yes, a part of her did.

Very much so.

A part of her wanted to tell him where he could shove his arrogant, presumptuous offer and head back to her hotel room and bury herself in the grief of today.

Yet the other part of Cat thrummed in suspense. Could she simply let loose and enjoy a night of passion with a very beautiful man with the cast-iron guarantee of no future?

It was refreshingly tempting.

He was seriously beautiful. Far more so than she was used to.

He was also rather more brusque and arrogant than she would choose, just rather too alpha for her.

She was tired, so tired of the inevitable let-down in relationships, the starting gun of hope, the numerous false starts and then the sprint that turned into an exhausting jog, and then standing bent, hands on thighs, and admitting defeat, because the two of you were just not going to make it to the finish line.

She was surprised at the ease of her decision.

'No.' Cat finally smiled. 'I have no problem with that.'

'Good.'

Housekeeping sorted, she tried to focus on the menu but, at thirty-four, she felt she'd just passed her driving test and been given the keys but was far from skilled enough to drive.

'Están listos para ordenar?'

The waiter came over and presumably asked if they were ready to order.

'I'll have paella.' She handed back the menu.

'The chicken here,' Dominic said, 'is the best you'll ever taste...'

Her eyes narrowed. Usually she'd say that she'd like the paella, thank you for interfering. She certainly didn't need a man choosing her food and yet as she glanced around, sure enough, the locals were eating the chicken.

Oh, he was so far from her usual fare but, no, he didn't need to be perfect tonight.

'When in Spain...' She shrugged.

She had the chicken and, as he had promised, it was amazing.

'Lemony, herby and so fat and juicy,' Cat commented on her second mouthful.

'And salty,' Dominic said. 'We'll be up all night, guz-zling water…'

He was presumptuous.

She knew, though, that he was right.

The rest of the world, the past, the future, was like rain as they huddled, as if under some imaginary um-brella, and enjoyed now—the spectacular food, the music that filled the restaurant.

They barely talked about work. She said something about being the only female consultant and how they gave every gynae patient to her. He mentioned how he'd lived in London till a couple of years ago, just half an hour or so away from her.

But then work got left behind and she found out how he loved the architecture in Edinburgh but was fast fall-ing in love with Spain.

And she told him about her passion for renovation, and her obsession with wallpaper, how she could spend hours leafing through sample books but, even then, you could never quite know how it would look once up.

Usually she never got to that part as eyes had long since glazed over with boredom.

His glazed with lust.

'Do you put it up yourself?' Dominic asked.

'I do.' She smiled.

'I feel emasculated.'

'Oh, I doubt you could ever be that.'

It was Dominic who then smiled.

Was it wrong? she wondered as they danced.

Was it wrong to be dancing and happy on his birthday?

Tonight it felt right.

A sexy flamenco dancer was kicking his heels and strumming away and then, when he slowed things down,

Cat felt her cheeks blaze with fire for sins not yet committed as Dominic pulled her into him.

His fingers ran lightly down her bare back and it felt utterly blissful.

'Fourteen hours later than I'd have preferred,' Dominic said into her ear, because that was how long it had been since he'd first itched for the feel of that sexy spine beneath his fingers.

'Well, I'm glad for your sake that you waited,' she said, imagining her reaction had he been so bold.

His touch didn't feel bold now; it felt right.

When the music ended they made it back to their table and when the bill came Cat did her usual and put her card down.

'We can go halves,' she said as he picked up the card to hand it back to her.

'Don't do that, Cat.'

'What?'

'Ruin a perfectly good night.'

If she were setting the ground rules for the future, she'd have insisted on paying her way.

Instead, they were setting the ground rules for tonight and she shivered in the warm night air as they headed for the hotel.

They walked back along the beach. It was after eleven but not really dark thanks to a near full moon and, despite the hour, the beach was far from deserted.

'There are some gorgeous beaches not far from here,' he said. 'Are you still determined to head back without seeing the place?'

'I am, though I wish I'd known just how much I'd like it,' she admitted. 'I'm going to come again but next time for a holiday. You're here a lot, then?'

'Quite a bit,' Dominic said. 'I have family here.'
'Oh.'

She ached to know more about him but Reticent was possibly his middle name because, apart from long conversations about everything and nothing, he gave away little.

The only thing she was sure of was their attraction.

'Which is why,' he continued, 'when I saw the conference was being held this year in Barcelona I decided to combine both. I'm very glad now that I did.' He turned her around and she looked into his dark eyes and his face. He was unreadable. 'I wish you had got here on Thursday.'

'Why?' she asked, her brain a bit sluggish with his mouth so close. She was far too used to focusing on work and she assumed that she must have missed some spectacular talk, or some cutting-edge revelation. The answer was far more basic than that.

'We could have had three nights instead of one.'

Still, he didn't kiss her, though she ached, *ached* for him to do so, but he just smiled in the dark like a beautiful devil and then they walked on.

Back at the hotel Cat was breathless, though not from walking, as they stepped into the foyer. They went through Reception and there was a lot of noise coming from the bar from their fellow attendees.

'Did you want to go to the bar?' Dominic offered.
'Yes.'
'Again,' he said, 'she lies.'
Cat smiled. 'She does.'
They headed for the elevators.
No, he didn't ask her for her floor.
He pressed his.

They stood backs against opposite walls facing each other as the lift groaned its way up, letting people in, letting people out.

And his eyes never left her face.

With three floors remaining they were finally alone and still he did not beckon.

Stay, Cat told herself, though she felt like a Labrador waiting for Christmas dinner.

Ping!

She walked slowly only because he did.

And his very steady hand swiped the card and opened the door to his room.

Would he offer her a drink? Cat wondered as she looked around.

The room was the same as hers, except it smelt of his cologne and there was a suitcase on the floor.

And then there was no time for further observation because he turned her to him and finally there was the bliss of his mouth. It was the roughest ever kiss and tasted divine. His tongue, his lips, his hands, the hunger in him was so consuming that there was no room for thought. She hadn't been kissed like this since—well, since for ever. His tongue was wicked, his hands pressing into her head and his body just primed and ready, because she could feel him.

She ached to feel him, so much so that the three garments of clothing she'd assumed he was wearing—was it only this morning?—were being unbuttoned and unzipped by Cat as his mouth never left her face.

He halted her briefly, long enough to retrieve his wallet, because of course he carried condoms, and she watched as he deftly put one on and so thick and hard was he that she played with him for a moment as he removed her dress.

She heard a brief tear and knew she would be up all week sewing Gemma's dress as it was now a white puddle on the floor.

She'd think about that later. Right now she was concentrating on him as his tongue met with her ear and she just about came in midair at the thought of him inside her.

Her bra was gone. She knew that because his mouth was on her breast as his hands slid her panties down.

And then she felt herself being lifted.

Not just onto him, but lifted out herself.

Out of grief, out of control, out of everything she knew.

Her shoulders met the wall and then he entered her and filled her, so rapidly and completely that it hurt enough to shout.

'Yes,' he said, and his mouth moved under her hair and his fingers met the back of her neck as he ground into her.

Cat wasn't used to being so thoroughly taken. A bit of foreplay might have been nice, but then she'd never been so close to coming in her life.

She was thoroughly rattled in the nicest of ways. He just kept thrusting in and she held on to her own hands behind his neck and then of her own accord was grinding down.

It felt amazing.

Just that.

It felt so amazing that he knew, more than she did herself, about what she liked.

Oh, she liked it rough.

She liked the intensity of him and the deep, rapid

thrusts and the way he stopped kissing her and stared her down.

He felt the tension and thank God for that because he was past consideration. He could feel the clamp of her thighs around him and the heat of her centre and had moved to the point of no return just as she started to pulse.

He loved orgasms, he met them regularly, but there was something so intense about hers, something so intrinsically matched to his, that she drove him on to more.

To get back to her mouth and rougher kisses and deeper thrusts and then he felt it, the slight collapse of her spinal column and the slump of her shoulders as she rested her head on his and he knew she was smiling.

Even as he shot the last of himself into her, he knew she was smiling and somehow that made him smile too.

No guilt, no regret, they met each other's eyes and kissed again but without haste this time.

Then he took her to bed and they lay there a moment before she was back to his mouth, down to his hips, and they did it all over again.

And again.

CHAPTER FOUR

DESPITE HAVING SLEPT for all of an hour, Dominic woke before sunrise.

Just as he always did.

Even if he went back to sleep afterwards, his body clock still dictated that he watch the sun come in.

He glanced at the clock and it was just after four and he knew where he needed to be.

Where they needed to be.

'Cat,' he said. 'Cat...' He watched her slowly stretch like her namesake. 'Get dressed...'

She could have, given the circumstances, assumed her use-by date had expired and she was being thrown out, but he gave her a kiss to awaken her and told her to hurry as he picked up the phone.

Her Spanish was...well, it wasn't, but she knew the word 'coffee' when she heard it in any language.

'Where are we going?' she asked as, doing up her espadrilles in the elevator, they made their way down.

'You need to see more of this city.'

'At 4:30 a.m.?'

'We could do it tomorrow if you'd stay another night.'

He hoped she would stay another night but they both knew that that wasn't happening.

Cat blinked as the doorman handed them two take-out coffees and Dominic took her hand and they walked to a car.

'You've hired a car.'

He didn't answer and when she got in she realised that it wasn't a hire car because there were coffee cups and papers and it looked pretty much like the inside of hers.

'Just how long are you here for?' she started to ask.

'Ask no questions,' he said.

Yes, she reminded herself, that was what they were about—fun, freedom…

And yet he intrigued her.

He spoke Spanish and he drove like a local through the dim city streets and she drank her coffee and tried to get her brain into gear.

'Come on.' He parked the car and took her hand and she was happy to just go with the adventure.

Without him she'd still be asleep.

Instead, she was wide-awake, walking up a hill and wondering just what the hell was going on, and then she remembered it was one of *those* days.

There was a tiny fracture to her mind, an angry inward curse that she could have made it through almost forty minutes of being awake without remembering the day that it was.

'This is Collserola,' Dominic explained. 'It is a national park—the green jewel of Barcelona…'

And it wasn't exclusively here for them because, as they climbed the hill, Cat found herself behind a group of tourists and it became clear as they chose their spot and sat on mossy ground that this was the place to be at sunrise.

And it was.

The city twinkled its night lights, the cars weaved in orange lines and beyond that, slowly, the dark ocean started to turn to blue as around them woodland came to life.

'It's amazing,' she said, and then turned to him but Dominic didn't answer.

He sat watching and tried to tell himself that he shouldn't have brought her, that he should feel guilt. Oh, there it was, this clutch of guilt in his chest had arrived. He had no issues with last night; it was the morning he was wrestling with.

And Cat didn't notice his lack of answer because as the world came to light she was on the edge of crying.

I miss you every single day.

I miss you this very second.

Just not every second.

Not every moment.

And sometimes moments run into hours but I still miss you every single day and will for ever.

How can that be? both wondered.

When did the seconds start to join up? When did that first full minute devoid of grief arrive and your leaving go unthought-of for an hour?

At what point did a cruel world start to turn beautiful again?

'To think I could have left without seeing this.' Cat broke the strange silence they were wrapped in and he turned then and looked at her.

And the clutch of guilt in his chest released.

It just went.

He would regret it later, Dominic decided.

Right now they shared a kiss.

A deep kiss that chased her softly to the ground and she could feel damp grass beneath bare shoulders and for them both all was right with the world.

It was a kiss unlike last night's, soft and tender, and she opened her eyes in the middle and saw his closed and wondered how it might be to be loved by this man.

It felt as if she was, it was the strangest glimpse of it. Her hands were in his hair and his mouth was still over hers, and if there hadn't been a lot of tourists present and two hundred cameras clicking, he would have made love to her, Cat knew.

He would have peeled off her dress and just slipped inside her.

She'd never come to a kiss, but the deep, sensual press of his mouth persisted. The roam of his hands was gentle, pressing into the side of her. In public, somehow shielded, she just came to private thoughts that she dared not examine and he nearly did too just feeling her slight rise and then the stillness in his arms.

It was a long, lingering kiss that had to stop and as his lips left hers she looked up into his eyes and she wished she could stay here for ever.

So did he.

Of course they couldn't.

'We have to get back,' he said, and waited for the clutch of guilt to return but it had escaped.

'We do.'

It was rather odd to step back into normality.

This time she pressed the lift button for her floor and there were others in there with them. When they arrived at her floor they shared a sort of odd wave as Cat got out.

Oh, my, she thought as she saw the damage to Gemma's dress. There were grass stains up the back, a tear near the bust, and then she looked at her face.

Yikes.

She looked as if she had spent the night having torrid sex with a stranger.

She had!

It was this morning that disconcerted her, though in the very nicest of ways.

She had a shower, wearing a shower cap, and then got out and picked half a forest out of her hair.

She had love bites on her breasts and she remembered his mouth there and suddenly she wanted him all over again.

She put on her lilac dress and went downstairs and took her seat in a talk she had been very much looking forward to.

But how did you concentrate on extracorporeal membrane oxygenation? Cat thought. Dominic was off doing whatever he was doing but he might as well have been sitting next to her because that's where her thoughts were.

She felt the buzz of her phone in her bag and she sneakily pulled it out.

Of course it couldn't be him, suggesting they sneak away, she reminded herself.

He didn't even know her number.

It just felt as if he should.

Instead, it was Gemma.

Are you okay?

Yes, but your dress isn't, Cat was tempted to reply. She thought of the tear he had made in it last night and the grass stains today.

She just hoped they had another one at Gatwick.

All good, Cat answered without thought, and then she guiltily fired another text.

It seems wrong to say that today.

She smiled when Gemma replied.

You awful person. Go to your room and be miserable this very minute. xxx

No, Cat didn't want to go to her room and cry away the day.

She closed her eyes.

She flew at seven and it seemed far, far too soon.

He wasn't around at lunchtime and thankfully Gordon was telling his story to someone else. There was a sag of disappointment in Cat, though, as she lined up for lunch, for the few remaining hours they were missing out on.

Still, there was always something to smile about and smile she did when she saw a lovely full silver platter of delectable paella and she held out her plate to the waiter.

'My room, now...'

She hadn't even heard him come up behind her and the low whisper in her ear was like an audible hallucination.

'I'm not going to get my paella, am I?' she said, but he'd gone.

No, she wasn't going to get her paella.

Two minutes later, with only sixteen minutes to spare before the afternoon session started, she was kneeling on the floor, hands splayed on his bed as he took her from behind.

He wasn't a considerate lover, just a very, very good one.

If they'd had time, Cat would have turned her head to tell him that usually she wouldn't...

Wouldn't what?

She did turn, though, and she saw his look of intense concentration, felt his fingers on her clitoris, urging her to come, and then she didn't even bother thinking. She just closed her eyes to the pleasure of being taken.

Her head was on her forearm and he was pounding her from behind and, Cat thought as she started to come, it was blissful to be that woman, even if just for a little while.

His.

They skipped the afternoon sessions.

Like bunking off school, they took his car again and drove for half an hour to a beach and sat there, eating ice cream and then rubbing suntan lotion into each other with sticky hands.

And on one of the saddest days in her calendar year she found bliss.

'So your parents are both doctors?' Dominic said as they lay on towels and stared at each other, and she nodded.

'Were they high achievers?'

'God, yes. They still are. It's easier to ring their secretaries to schedule lunch than try to do it myself.'

'You are joking?' he checked.

'Half.' She smiled. 'What about yours?'

He seemed to think before answering.

He was.

They really hadn't spoken about anything other than themselves but it felt quite normal to have her ask.

'I don't really know where to start,' he admitted. 'Well, my mother never worked. Her sole job was to look beautiful for my father. He was an arrogant bastard. Growing up, I hardly ever saw him—he worked on the stock market and would bring his stress home, worrying about the yen or the pound dropping a quarter of a percentage point.' Her eyes were so patient, Dominic thought. She didn't ask questions; she just lay there, staring.

Because she loved his voice.

Because anything he said she wanted to hear.

'Anyway, then he had the absolute fortune of collapsing with a heart attack and going into full cardiac arrest.'

'Fortune?'

'We always joke now that he had a personality transplant because, while his illness made me switch from physics to biology and suddenly become very interested in medicine and saving the world, my father completely changed. He was very depressed at first and he had to see a psychologist and things but then he completely turned his life around. He sold up, got out of the money game, and he and my mother fell in love all over again, and now...'

He hesitated. He didn't want to give too many specifics. He didn't want to say that he was looking forward to Monday and heading over to see his slightly eccentric parents or rather, disconcertingly, he did want to tell her just that.

There was a part of Dominic that wanted to extend this conversation, which meant extending them, and that wasn't what this weekend was about so he kept things light.

'They started an internet dating service. Or rather it wasn't by internet initially, it was more a word-of-mouth thing. They used to set up their friends and anyone coming over to Spain...'

'Stop!' Cat laughed.

'It's true, though. Now they run this very exclusive dating site for the over fifties...'

To hear this rather detached man talking about his crazy parents made Cat start to *really* laugh.

Oh, she laughed at times, of course she did.

Just not like this.

They lay then in silence and Dominic thought about the six months after Heather had died.

After the funeral, instead of throwing himself into work, as had been his initial plan, he had accepted his parents' suggestion to come and stay in Spain with them.

At first they had infuriated him with their calm acceptance of the terrible facts. Of course they had been upset but not once had they matched his anger.

As he had raged and paced around the villa, or slept in well past midday, they had simply accepted him and whatever place he was in—providing conversation when needed and meals that appeared whether he felt he needed them or not.

And finally, when the anger had gone, Dominic had been very grateful for their presence and calm, which had allowed him to heal in his own time.

He had spent days walking and watching the ocean as he slowly come back to join a world that had altered for ever. Yet move on he had, catching himself the first time he'd found himself laughing along at a joke or smiling at a thought that had popped into his head.

And a smile stretched his lips as he thought of them now.

'They're amazing people,' he admitted. 'So, yes, what seemed like the most terrible disaster at the time turned out to be a blessing.'

They stared at each other, they found each other, right there in that moment.

'Don't leave tonight…' he said, but even before the words were out he was changing his mind and even as she heard them there was confusion in her eyes because it was supposed to be a one-night stand.

'Come on,' he said. 'Let's go in the water.'

There they could be apart and think.

There she could work out how to articulate the million reasons that she had to go back. How did she tell him that the woman he had met this weekend didn't actually exist, that she wasn't floaty and feminine and spontaneous?

She was rigid and brittle and meticulous.

And Dominic too, as they ran to the water, was wondering what had possessed him to ask her to stay.

But not even the sea could keep them apart because ten strides in they were waist deep in water, limbs around each other, kissing in the sun, out on display, and there was no reason in the world why she should leave.

The water was idyllic, just a shade cooler than the temperature of skin, and she could feel the sun beating on her shoulders.

She'd heard about the magical seven. Seven waves in, seven out, seven years since love had died and today it felt as if it was being born again.

They said nothing but their kisses were deep and tender but whatever they were finding was invaded, whatever the moment had meant it was gone.

'*Ayuda!*'

No, Cat didn't know Spanish, but a cry for help she was familiar with and she swung around.

'*Necesito ayuda...*'

Dominic was already swimming over to an elderly man who was waving his arms. Beside him on a pedalo there was a woman who was sitting up but even from here Cat could see she was in trouble. She was clutching her chest and leaning forward.

Others were coming over to assist and Dominic was calling out to a woman standing on the beach to call for an ambulance.

He called for Cat to go to shore. 'In my backpack!' he shouted. 'There's a pack...'

At least someone was organised today.

Cat raced up the beach as a group of men steered the pedalo in and then carried the woman to the shore.

She was still sitting up, Cat noted as she shook the contents of his backpack out.

There it was, a small pack, but as she went to stuff the contents she had tipped out back inside, her hand closed on a small bump in his wallet.

A circular bump.

She shook her head and ran back towards the gathered crowd.

'Thanks...'

She opened the pack. There were gloves, a mouth-guard and airway... There was even a small kit for IV access and she watched his very steady hands slip a needle in, all the while reassuring the woman, who was clammy and sweaty, that she would be okay.

It should feel very different to be out in the middle of nowhere rather than in the calm efficiency of the emergency department, yet he had everything under control—a few beachgoers were holding their towels to shade the woman from the fierce afternoon sun and Dominic wiped her face with a cloth soaked in bottled water and spoke calming words in Spanish.

Cat noticed he was holding the woman's wrist as he spoke, keeping a constant watch on her pulse. As she glanced down at Dominic's hand Cat wondered if she had been blind or simply not looked, because now she could see the slight pinkness of a ring mark on his suntanned skin.

She felt a bit sick.

In the distance she could hear sirens and, even if the worst happened now and the lady went into cardiac arrest, assistance and equipment were just a few moments away.

The paramedics were just as efficient as they were back home and rather more used to retrieving heavy patients from a sun-drenched sandy beach than they would be in London.

They spoke at length with Dominic as they did the ECG tracing and administered analgesia and generally made the woman more comfortable before transferring her onto the stretcher.

The men all carried the stretcher up the beach until they let the legs down on the stony ground.

Her heart was racing, not from the mild drama but from what she had thought she had felt.

A wedding ring?

Surely not, Cat thought.

But why not? another voice in her head asked.

Why the hell not?

'Let's grab our things and head back,' Dominic said, and she nodded and tried not to shrug him off as his arm went around her waist.

She didn't know what to say to him. She just didn't know how to speak.

'You've caught the sun,' he commented as they drove back to the hotel.

'I know,' she said. Her shoulders were stinging but not as much as her thoughts.

'Are you okay?' Dominic checked.

'Of course.' She cleared her throat. 'It was just a bit upsetting.'

'What?' He glanced over. 'She had chest pain.'

Oh, that's right. Cat remembered the man she had disliked before she had completely fallen under his spell. He was arrogant, dismissive and rather mean.

'It's different without all the equipment...'

He didn't comment. Chest pain was such a routine part of his day and he'd assumed it was the same for her.

'She'll be fine,' he said, but she couldn't answer.

They were back in the elevators and she went to push the button for her floor but his hand stopped her and he pushed his.

Arrogant bastard, Cat thought this time.

Still, she wanted to be sure so she went with him to his hotel room and, completely at ease, he dropped his clothes and headed for the shower.

She didn't join him.

He washed off the sand and was glad that she hadn't come in. He needed to think.

Was he going to ask again that she stay awhile longer?

And if she couldn't, was he going to ask to see her again?

'What time is your flight?' he called from the shower.

'Seven,' she answered, and then she did something most uncharacteristic for her. She wasn't a nosy person yet she was about this.

She went into his bag and pulled out his wallet and opened it, and she didn't need to dig for the ring to find her answer. She pulled out a photo instead.

Cat knew her fashion and, yep, this was pretty recent.

Dominic made a lovely groom.

He also made a very dark lover because she jumped when she heard his voice.

'I wish you hadn't done that, Cat.'

He stood with a towel around his waist, watching as she tucked the photo back in. In his mind he was conflicted.

Tell her.

No.

Because then the bubble burst and everything they had found this weekend dispersed.

Yes, he could explain.

He simply wasn't ready to.

If he was going to tell her, then it would be in his own time.

And their time had run out.

He didn't like a snoop.

'Do you know what, Dominic?' She looked up at him. The delicious scent of him, fresh from the shower, was reaching her now and she practically held her breath as she gave a grim smile. 'I wish I hadn't done that either.'

She tossed the wallet on the bed and walked past him.

And he held open the door and let her out.

CHAPTER FIVE

Cat arrived back at Gatwick Airport and, of course, because she didn't need it now, her suitcase was amongst the first to come out.

Instead of driving home, though, she found herself on a search of the shops and thankfully found Gemma's dress.

They met in the canteen on Monday morning and Cat got back her photo while Gemma received the second version of the white dress.

'Thank you so much for this.' Gemma beamed as she peered into the bag. 'It's beautiful, isn't it? I know I probably shouldn't wear white for the christening...'

'It's not a wedding,' Cat said. 'You don't have to worry about offending the bride.'

She looked at the dress as Gemma pulled out a corner and she felt her throat go tight. Hers, she knew, should have been thrown straight into the garbage but instead she'd thrown it into the back of her wardrobe.

No, she wanted to say to Gemma, *I did not have sexual relations with that married man.*

Oh, help.

She most certainly had.

'So how was it?' Gemma asked.

'It was great,' Cat said. 'Very informative.'

'About what?'

'Well,' Cat attempted, 'about things.'

'And how was your talk?'

'It went really well,' she said, but all she could really remember of it was the moment Dominic had walked into the room and how he had stood with his arms folded at the back.

'And how was the museum?'

Cat frowned.

'You said you were going to do some sightseeing and go to the museum, maybe get a bit of inspiration for your bedroom.'

As Cat's cheeks burned pink, she wondered if her friend was a witch.

'Well, did you?'

'Did I what?'

'Get inspiration for the bedroom?'

'No.'

'Oh.'

'And no shopping for stuffed donkeys, I see.'

'I was working, Gemma.'

'Of course you were.' Gemma smirked.

She knew, Cat was quite sure.

Had she examined things more carefully at the time, some flags might have been raised. Perhaps it should have been obvious, Cat thought, that he was married. Yet his reluctance to share personal information hadn't been an issue at the time; instead, it had felt as if they were chasing the same thing—fun, pleasure, grabbing the moment and running with it.

It had started to feel different at Collserola, though.

Cat couldn't properly explain it but there she had

started to want more than just the weekend. There, watching the sunrise, there had been a shift and she had felt him pensive beside her and for a moment, just a moment, she had felt as if time might not have been running out for them.

And that night, her second without him, Cat did what she'd tried not to because it hurt too much—she recalled their kiss in the sea. For a while there she'd thought she'd be staying.

Not for ever.

Just that something had been starting.

Something far bigger than either had expected to find.

Yet, as guilty as she felt about the weekend, Cat didn't feel used—after all, she had gone along with the anonymity that had been offered. She had enjoyed embracing her femininity, going out and doing things she never would have done had Dominic not been there.

And, even though she did her level best to forget him, their time together could not be undone and it was as if he had set off a little chain reaction, because colour started coming back into her life.

The following Sunday Cat wore another new dress to the twins' christening, a burnt orange and red paisley wraparound dress, and her hair was worn down and curly.

Glynn had rung to apologise and explain that his mother had been taken ill and Cat had had a difficult time explaining to him that, no, she wasn't not coming to see him because of what had happened. 'I like it curly, Glynn,' Cat said. 'Of course I'll be in again...'

Just not yet.

For now she enjoyed having those two extra hours a week not having her hair yanked and blown smooth.

She stood at the font, looking at Gemma's dress as she and Nigel juggled the twins, and wondering who on earth she was to offer guidance as a godmother, while knowing if that day ever came, then she would.

Oh, she doubted she would ever marry but she did believe in the sanctity of it and to think about what had happened made a curl of shame inside her that meant it was something she wouldn't be discussing with Gemma.

She loved Gemma and Nigel and their little family and she remembered Thomas's christening and when they had been there for her.

Gemma must have been thinking of it too, because she gave her friend the nicest smile and later pulled her aside.

'My parents are driving me crazy,' Gemma said. 'They want to know when we're having the cake. I'm sure they want to go home.'

Cat smiled. Gemma's parents loathed any change to their routine.

'Are you okay, Cat?'

'Of course.'

They told each other everything and she could have come up with some airy excuse, that today was hard because…

Only, she wouldn't use Thomas as an excuse for not being able to meet her friend's eyes.

'What are you up to, Cat?'

'I'm not up to anything.'

'Is there something you're not telling me?'

For the first time since they'd been teenagers she lied properly to her friend.

'Don't be daft.'

And she got on with smiling and enjoying this very special day.

But over the next few weeks Cat threw herself into her work and studying for her exams, which were tough but no tougher than expected. It meant there was no time to catch up with Gemma.

And even when three weeks' annual leave stretched ahead of her, she still avoided her friend.

Though she was starting to realise that she wouldn't be able to avoid her for long.

Gemma texted.

Is everything okay?

Cat didn't answer.
Gemma persisted.

Did we have an argument that I didn't notice?

Finally Cat texted back.

Can I tell you when I'm ready?

Because she wasn't just yet.

Of course.

No, she wasn't quite ready, so she stripped walls and sanded back a mantelpiece and tried to face something she was avoiding.

When it proved too hard, she took herself to her

favourite shop and spent a morning turning pages of wallpaper samples.

'I think a silver grey,' Cat said to Veronica, the owner, who was as obsessed with wallpaper as she was. 'Perhaps with one wall in silver and the rest in a matt finish…'

Silver moonlight hues had appealed but as Veronica went to clear some space so they could put together samples she moved a book and suddenly it wasn't those colours that Cat wanted.

'I haven't seen this,' she said.

'It's only just in…'

'Oh, my,' Cat said. She could almost feel the pulse from the sample book as she turned the pages. It was like being walked blindfolded and then having it re-moved and finding herself standing in a spring park. Birds, butterflies and tree branches that stretched and flowers, endless flowers…

It reminded her of Collserola and that one magical morning and she certainly didn't need such a constant reminder, except…

'Would this be a feature wall?' Cat checked, and then almost winced when the assistant pulled up some im-ages on her computer screen.

Every wall was covered. In some of the images even the ceilings were papered. It was a sort of cross between a cheap Paris hotel and an enchanted wood.

'This is so far removed from what I was planning,' Cat said, and Veronica nodded.

'You don't want to know the price.'

'I don't,' Cat said, and tried to get back to silver grey. 'Have you got it in?'

'I do, though it's incredibly hard to get hold of. It

was on a special order but the buyer couldn't wait and went for something less…'

'Less what?' Cat asked. 'Less migraine inducing, less…?' She let out a breath. 'Less sexy…?'

Yes, somehow it was sexy.

'Just less,' Veronica said.

It was sold to the guilty conscience that just wanted to revisit that gorgeous morning over and over again.

A time when the world had been absolutely beautiful.

Magical even.

The strange thing, Cat thought as she stepped back a full week later and surveyed her handiwork, the world still was.

Magical.

Instead of the muted tones for the bedroom she had chosen colour. And now, in autumn, she stood in the middle of summer and imagined this being her haven when winter came in.

Yes, that weekend had changed her in a way she was finally accepting.

'Hey, Gemma.' Cat called her friend, who had so patiently waited for the morose mood to pass by. 'The bedroom's finished.'

Gemma really was a brilliant friend. She came over within an hour, clutching a bottle of champagne and two glasses, and they did a walk through the house. Cat had a photo in each room of what it had looked like before she'd set to work and it was hard to believe now just how bad it had once been.

As she opened the bedroom door she watched her friend's jaw drop in absolute amazement as she stepped in.

'I want to live in your bedroom for ever,' Gemma said.

'Nigel might not be too pleased.'

'He can come too,' Gemma said. 'Oh, my, it is beauti-ful. It's just stunning. I can't believe you've finished the house.'

'I haven't yet.'

'Well, it looks pretty perfect to me. What do you still have left to do—the garden?'

'No.'

Gemma followed Cat out of the master bedroom and down the hallway that no longer creaked when you walked, and she frowned as Cat opened up the guest bedroom.

It had a dark wooden bed that was dressed in white linen. There was a gorgeous bookcase next to the open fire. On the mantelpiece were beautiful ornaments. Every last piece had been chosen with care.

'But it's already perfect,' Gemma said.

'I'm going to make it into a nursery.'

'Will it sell better if you do?

'No, I've decided against selling.'

'So why are you making it into…?' The penny was slowly dropping and a rather stunned Gemma halted and turned to her friend.

Yes, there was magic in nature.

'You're pregnant?'

There was a long stretch of silence.

Gemma was an obstetrician and she was used to women finding themselves rather unexpectedly pregnant.

It seemed today, though, that it was the doctor who was more surprised.

She was.

Cat had spent the past few weeks fighting the idea and then getting used to it. A private person, she revealed only when she was ready.

And tonight she was.

'How long have you known?' Gemma asked.

'A couple of weeks after the twins were christened,' Cat said. 'I tried to put it out of my mind, what with my exams and everything. I decided to work out how I felt when I was on leave.'

'And how do you feel?' Gemma asked, struggling to put back on her obstetrician's hat.

'Well, I'm going to be terrified until I have the tests and get all the results back…'

'The chances of it happening again are minimal,' Gemma said.

'I know they are.'

'But you shan't relax till they're in.' Gemma smiled gently and Cat nodded. 'Apart from that, how do you feel?'

'I still don't know,' Cat admitted. 'I don't know if I'm happy or worried or anything really.'

'You know that I'm here for you, whatever you decide.'

'I do and even if I haven't been ready to speak about it till now, it's helped a lot to know that.'

Gemma opened the champagne.

For herself.

She didn't even bother with a glass!

'What about Rick? How did he take it?'

'It isn't Rick's.'

'Then who—'

'I don't want to discuss that.'

'Now, hold on a minute,' Gemma said. 'You're not my patient yet—you're my friend so we *are* going to discuss that. What happened in Spain?'

'How do you know that it was in Spain?'

'Because you've been different since then, and also you don't top up your tan by sitting in a hotel room.'

'Yes, it was then,' Cat admitted. 'I met someone but it was never going to be going anywhere. It was supposed to be a bit of fun, a weekend of no consequence...' She gave a wry smile. 'We were careful...'

'You have no idea how many times I hear that a day,' Gemma said.

'We used condoms.'

'Note the plural,' Gemma said. 'Was it a sex-fest, then?'

'I guess.'

'You dirty girl.' Gemma grinned.

'Okay, I can tell you what happened now.' And so she told Gemma all about the hair appointment that hadn't happened and the missing luggage. 'I ended up wearing your dress for the presentation,' Cat explained. 'I felt like a fish out of water at first but then I started to enjoy myself. I felt a bit like my old self. Anyway, he made it very clear from the start that he was only interested in the weekend and nothing more...' Cat thought about the moment when he had asked her to stay on for longer but she shoved that aside. It didn't matter now. 'At first I was going to tell him to get lost, he's not my usual type at all, but then...' She shrugged. 'I decided that a weekend of no-strings fun was better than six months of starting out all hopeful and then slowly finding out that a relationship wasn't working.'

'And was it?'

'For a while,' Cat said.

'So, what's his name?'

'Dominic,' she replied.

'And have you told him about the baby?' Gemma asked.

'He's married.' Cat made herself say it. They stood

in the spare room that would soon be a nursery in silence. It was Cat who broke it. 'I'm sorry, Gemma…'

'You don't have to say sorry to me,' Gemma said. 'After all, it wasn't Nigel who you slept with.'

'I know, but even so.' There were tears in Cat's eyes. She still couldn't quite believe how careless she'd been. 'I didn't know that he was married right until the end— the bastard had taken off his ring and tucked it in his wallet. I probably didn't ask enough questions,' she admitted. 'He seemed very direct to me. He didn't seem the sort of person who would cheat, which says a lot about my gauge for guys…'

'Well, whether he's married or not,' Gemma said, and Cat knew that her friend's doctor's hat was firmly on now, 'Dominic still has a responsibility towards the baby…'

Cat shook her head. 'It might be a bit late to be thinking of it but I'm not tearing a family apart. I'm not going to contact him just yet. I don't even know where he works, I don't even know his surname…'

'Come off it, Cat.'

'Okay, I looked up the conference attendees and I do know his surname but I can manage—'

'It's actually not about you and whether or not you can manage,' Gemma said. 'And it's not about his wife and how she'll react. It's about the baby, Cat.' Gemma was as firm as Cat had known she would be. The very questions that she had been wrestling with for weeks were now being voiced by her friend. 'It's about your baby, who will grow up and will want to know, and has a right to know, who their father is. Whether or not you want him to be, Dominic has a right to be involved, or not, in his baby's life.'

'I know all of that,' Cat said. 'And I shall tell him, just not yet. Gemma, I'm eleven weeks pregnant. I'm doing my very best to simply get used to that fact. I'm not going to upend his life while I'm still in my first trimester...'

'Oh, but you'll upend yours. Why the hell should he get away with a few weeks of stress—'

'I'm not stressed,' Cat said. 'I was at first but I'm not now. I want this baby and I'm going to do the very best that I can by it. I shall look up Dominic at some point but not now. Not now while I'm still trying to work things out. I need to find out the test results before I tell anyone. I need to know that it's not going to be happening again...'

Cat knew she had Gemma's support and, yes, she could tell her most things but there was something she couldn't explain to her friend just yet because she didn't actually understand it herself.

She missed Dominic.

Yes, it had been but one weekend and, yes, she was angry, not just with him but herself.

It was how she would react when she saw him that terrified Cat.

She knew that she wouldn't cry and break down if he told her he wanted nothing to do with them—it would come as a relief, in fact.

And she didn't want a penny from him either.

There were two things that terrified her—how he might react to the news if their baby was less than perfect, which was understandable given all that had gone on.

And how she might react if he took the news well.

Or, rather, how she might react when she saw him again.

What if that spark blew all her scruples away?
The mere thought of his kisses terrified her.
His smooth talk too.
She had this awful glimpse of life as a mistress.
Tucked away in England with her baby.
And she'd never be that.
If he was to be in their baby's life, then it would be without lies.
Which meant someone was going to get hurt.

CHAPTER SIX

CAT DID LOOK him up.

At twenty weeks gestation, when her scan and amnio had come through as clear, Gemma told her that she had no excuse not to.

It really had been an excuse because whatever the outcome of the tests it wouldn't have changed the course of the pregnancy for Cat.

But the results came in before Christmas and Cat had visions of Dominic and his fraught wife and the triplets she had now assigned to him, and decided she couldn't ruin Christmas for them.

Or New Year.

Still, she had looked him up and it had taken about fifteen minutes to find out where he worked.

She recalled him saying that he liked the architecture in Edinburgh and after a few false starts she found someone who knew him and was told he was now working at a large teaching hospital in Glasgow.

Ah, that's right, Cat remembered, he didn't like to be tied to one place for too long.

Or one person.

And so Cat had sat on that knowledge for another month.

Her second pregnancy threw up so many memories

of her first. There were so many thoughts and fears and she wanted to get past the milestone she had reached with Thomas.

Finally, though, she plucked up the courage to make the call.

'You're looking for Mr Edwards?' A cheery female voice, with a heavy Glaswegian accent, checked.

'Dominic Edwards—he's an emergency consultant.'

'Oh, you mean Dom!' There was a long pause. 'No, he was only here for a couple of months... Sorry, I've no idea where he is now.'

And that ended that.

Though, not quite, of course.

Now into February and thirty weeks pregnant Cat and Gemma caught up one Monday morning for breakfast in the canteen. They were interviewing for Cat's maternity leave position and she didn't want to be around for that.

Pregnancy suited her and she was enjoying this one. Colour had continued to come back into her life since that weekend and she was wearing the paisley dress that she had bought for the twins' christening, along with chocolate-brown high-heeled boots. Her hair hadn't been straightened since and hung over her shoulder in a thick, long ponytail.

'I really don't want to see who's replacing me,' she admitted as she peeled the lid of her yoghurt and, having licked it, added, 'Temporarily, of course! I'll be back.'

'Full-time?' Gemma checked.

'That was the plan,' Cat admitted, 'and I've told Andrew that I shall be returning full-time but I'm starting to really wonder how on earth I'm going to manage it.'

'Have they had many applicants for the role?' Gemma asked.

'There have been a few, but only two standouts—two women who are looking at job share,' Cat said.

'You could think about doing that,' Gemma suggested.

'I don't like sharing at the best of times and especially not my job,' Cat said. 'Still, I'm going to have to work something out. I can't believe how quickly my due date is coming up.'

Cat had always heard women saying that their pregnancy seemed to drag on for ever, yet hers seemed to be galloping along at breakneck speed.

Work was as unrelenting as ever and she did her level best not to bring any aches and pains with her, but by the end of the day she was exhausted. The nursery hadn't been sorted out; instead, her days off were spent looking at child-care centres. All to no avail. Even the crèche at the hospital wasn't geared to a baby whose single parent worked such erratic hours.

'If I'm going to work, then I'm going to have to get a nanny,' Cat conceded as she added sugar to her tea. 'But even that comes with its own set of problems.'

'Such as?'

'I have a two-bedroom home.' She sighed. 'A small two-bedroom home.'

'And you don't like sharing.' Gemma smiled. 'Can't you get somewhere bigger?'

'I'm going to have to at some stage but the thing is, I love my home. I've just got it exactly how I want it but, yes, I guess I'm going to have to look at moving. Not yet, though,' she said. 'I think I'll stay put for now and once I've had the baby I'll think about putting the house on the market. I'll have six months to move…'

'So you're planning to have your house on the market, find another one *and* move, all with a new baby?'

'It's a baby,' Cat said. 'I'm not going to be working...' She let out a sigh. 'I haven't got a clue, have I?'

'Well, if anyone could do it all, then it would be you,' Gemma said. 'Though I just can't imagine how I'd have managed when the twins were tiny. Just having people viewing the house when you're trying to feed or you've just got...' Gemma hesitated '...*it* off to sleep...'

'You were about to say *him*.' Cat smiled.

'No, I wasn't,' Gemma refuted. 'What I'm actually trying to say is that I wouldn't count on getting too much done during those six months of maternity leave. It's isn't an extended holiday, Cat. If you are considering moving to somewhere bigger, it might be a good idea to start that ball rolling now...'

'I guess.' She sighed. 'Even if the new place does need some work, I could do that while I'm...' She stopped when she saw Gemma's small eyebrow rise and then laughed. 'Okay, I'm going to accept that I have no real idea as to the disruption this small person is going to make to my life when *he* arrives.' Cat waited for Gemma to comment but she didn't. 'I want to find out what I'm having.'

'Well, then, it's good that you've got an appointment to see me this evening.'

'Gemma!' Cat protested, because now that she had made up her mind, she wanted to know straight away. 'Tell me.'

'No, I won't tell you here and I'm serious about that. We agreed that catch-ups were for friend talk and my office was for official baby talk...'

'Fair enough,' she grumbled.

'And speaking as a friend and not a doctor, have you—'

'I need to get back,' Cat interrupted. She didn't want to get into that conversation with Gemma *again*, and explain that she still hadn't spoken with Dominic.

She knew, though, that she needed to contact him.

Tonight, she decided, she'd deal with it tonight but almost immediately she changed her mind.

It was surely better to ring around hospitals during the day. It would sound far more professional to any of his colleagues than calling at night, and she certainly didn't want to create gossip for him.

Gemma started to head to Outpatients, where she was holding antenatal clinics all day, and Cat would be her last patient. 'I'll see you at five. Hopefully I shan't be running late. Come and have dinner after,' she suggested. 'We might even make it in time to see the twins before they go down for the night.'

'I'd love that. I honestly don't know how you do it,' Cat admitted. 'Do you feel like you're missing out?'

'Sometimes.' Gemma nodded. 'I worry more, though, that they're missing out on me and so I completely overcompensate when I do see them and rot up all of Nigel's routines. I know I'm lucky, though. I don't have to worry about them while I'm here and I can concentrate on work, knowing that they're at home with their dad.' She gave her friend a smile. 'You need your own Nigel.'

Cat smiled back but the thing was, she didn't want her own Nigel.

She wanted… Cat halted her thoughts right there. Dominic wasn't the man she thought she had met. And even if he was, it was supposed to have been a one-night stand. He had said to her face that he didn't want to be tied to any one person or place. She couldn't really imagine his reaction when he found out that she was having his baby.

She didn't want his reaction.

Cat slowed down her walking. There was a flutter of panic in her chest as she remembered her last pregnancy and the disappointment of Thomas's father, the silent suggestion of blame for daring to mess up his perfect life.

She didn't want that for herself again and she couldn't stand it for her baby.

Yet she had to.

She was tired of the guilt that came with putting it off and she decided that, bar an emergency coming into the department, she wasn't leaving her office until she had found out where he was working and had contacted him.

Did she tell him outright? Cat wondered.

Suggest that they meet?

So deep in her thoughts was she that at first she didn't notice the tall suited man walking alongside Andrew.

He noticed her, though.

In fact, at first sight she barely looked pregnant.

She was wearing a tight dress and high boots and looked somehow sexy and elegant but then she turned to speak with one of the nurses and he saw the tight, round swell of her stomach and, attempting a detached professional guess, he would put her at…

Yes, there was something that they needed to discuss. That was why he was here after all.

He watched as she turned from the conversation she was having and startled as she glanced towards him, but then she gave a small shake of her head and strode on.

Then she looked over towards him again and he watched as not only did her face pale but she stood frozen to the spot.

Frozen.

For a foolish moment Cat considered darting into a cubicle—it would be a futile game of hide-and-seek, though, because it would appear that she'd already been found.

And so, as Andrew called her over, somehow she did her best to pretend that the walls of the emergency department weren't shaking and that the ground wasn't opening up between her feet.

She walked towards him.

Dominic.

Her one-night stand.

The father of her child.

'Cat.' Andrew beamed. 'Did you have nice days off?'

'I did.'

'Excellent! I tried not to worry you, but on Friday one of the job share applicants pulled out and the other wasn't interested in pursuing the position if she couldn't be guaranteed regular part-time hours.'

'I see,' Cat said, even though she didn't.

'I've still got two more interviews to complete,' Andrew went on, although Cat knew those two were really more of a formality and would be a rather poor choice. 'However,' Andrew said, 'we had a late applicant. Cat, this is Dominic Edwards. He's been working in Scotland for the last two years but we're hoping to lure him back south of the border.'

For now, Cat knew, she would simply have to go along with the polite small talk. Whatever the reason Dominic was here, whatever the outcome when she told him her news, at the first opportunity she would have a quiet word with Andrew. Hopefully she wouldn't have to reveal to her colleague that Dominic was her baby's father, but if she had to, then she would. There was no way this could happen.

No way!

Thankfully there was a call for help from one of the cubicles and Cat was just about to flee in relief and go and assist when Andrew halted her. 'I'll go,' he said. 'If you could carry on showing Dominic around.'

'I can deal with the patient,' Cat said. 'You're in the middle of conducting an interview.'

'I know, but the patient happens to be my mother-in-law.' Andrew rolled his eyes. 'The interview has already been interrupted twice. My apologies again, Dominic...'

'It's no problem at all,' Dominic said. 'Take your time.'

As Andrew walked off Cat stood there and she truly didn't know what to say.

She kept praying that the alarm clock would buzz, or that there would be a knock on the door to the on-call room and she'd find out she was having a bad dream.

A vaguely sexy bad dream, though, because rather inappropriately, given the circumstances, she couldn't help but notice how amazing he looked.

When in Spain, the times that he'd had clothes on, Dominic had dressed smartly, though somewhat more casually than he was now. Today, on a Monday morning, he seemed too beautiful for the rather scruffy emergency department. Dressed in a dark grey suit and tie, his hair was shorter than she remembered but it still had enough length that it fell forward. Clean shaven, he smelt as he had the last time she had seen him, the moment he had stepped out of the shower.

The moment she had walked away and he hadn't stopped her—in fact, he had held the door open.

And, just like that day, she could feel his contained anger.

'Has the cat got your tongue, Cat?' he asked as she stood in silence.

It would seem that it had because still she said nothing.

'Well, I'll make this very simple for you, then,' he pushed on. 'A, B or C?'

Cat could feel her eyelashes blink rapidly as he sped through the multi-choice he had created just for her.

'A—mine, B—not mine, or C—not sure.'

'Dominic…' she said, and how strange it felt to be saying his name while looking at him again. How odd it felt that he was here, terribly beautiful, terribly cross. 'It's not that simple…' Cat attempted. But it was to him.

'A, B or C, Cat?'

She couldn't meet his eyes as she delivered the answer. 'A.'

'Mine.'

Yours.

His.

Dominic said nothing at first. He tried to stare her down but she refused to look at him as she now attempted to speak.

'I was going to try to find out where you were working. Today, in fact,' Cat said.

'I don't believe you for a moment.'

She couldn't blame him for that.

'What time to do you finish work?' Dominic asked.

'I've got plans tonight,' Cat said to his shoulder, because she still couldn't meet his eyes.

'Tough,' he said. 'Cancel them.'

'I've actually got a doctor's appointment.'

He hesitated but he refused to be fobbed off. 'What time is your appointment?'

'Five,' Cat said. 'But my obstetrician is a friend of mine and I'm going there for dinner afterwards…' She was floundering for excuses. She would far prefer to have had this conversation over the phone or via email. There at least she could have hidden from his angry gaze.

And, yes, he was angry—even if she was doing her best not to see it, she could feel it from his stance and she could hear it in his terse voice.

'I'm quite sure that your obstetrician friend will understand that you can't make dinner because you're going to be having a long overdue conversation with your baby's…' He halted and glanced over her shoulder, and Cat guessed that Andrew was making his way back.

'Name somewhere,' Dominic said, 'and I'll be there.'

She hesitated a beat too long for his impatient mood.

'Name somewhere,' he said again, 'or I'll just keep right on talking until you do and your boss will quickly realise that I have a rather vested interest in this maternity leave position.'

'Oliver's,' Cat said, referring to a small wine bar that a lot of staff at the hospital frequented. 'It's just down the—'

'I'm sure that I'm capable of working it out.'

The conversation ended as Andrew joined them again.

'How's your mother-in-law?' Dominic asked politely.

'Thankfully, she's about to head off to the ward.' Andrew gave a sigh of relief. 'Would you like to come and take a look at the radiology department, Dominic?'

'I'd love to,' he said, and then he addressed Cat. 'It was nice to meet you.'

'And you.' She gave him a tight smile.

For the next couple of hours Dominic remained in the department, being shown around, observing a clinic and being introduced to staff. It was clear to Cat that Andrew had decided that he had the role.

She was busy enough to avoid him and Dominic seemed fine with that for he made no attempt to catch her eye or talk.

He did let her know, though, when he was leaving. She was sitting on a high stool, trying to write up some notes, but had just put her hands on her hips to curve her aching back and stretch it when he came in.

'I'm heading off,' he said, and Cat glanced around and saw that they were alone.

'You don't have to tell me your movements,' she responded in a very crisp voice. Now that the shock of seeing him was starting to wear off, her own anger with him was making itself known and she let a little of it out. 'You knew full well that I worked here. What on earth were you thinking?'

'We'll speak tonight,' he said. 'Take as long as you need for your appointment but don't even think of not showing up afterwards. I want this sorted before we start working together.'

'Working together?' she checked. 'I thought you were applying for the maternity leave position.'

'I am but Andrew mentioned that you were short-staffed and wanted to know how I'd feel about doing a few locum shifts prior to commencing full-time.'

'*If* you get the job.'

'Why wouldn't I get it? The interview went very

well,' he said. 'I happen to be very good at what I do. Andrew seems to think I'd be an asset…'

He'd be an emotional liability, though, Cat thought. Well, she'd soon see about him working here, she decided as Dominic stalked off, though she didn't get a chance to speak to Andrew for the rest of the day.

Instead, she sat in Gemma's office at a quarter to six, having her blood pressure taken. Given who had just arrived on the scene, neither Gemma nor Cat were surprised to find that it was a smudge high.

'I can't believe that he'd just show up like that,' Cat said as her friend undid the cuff.

'Well, I think it's a good thing that it's all being brought to a head,' Gemma said. 'Go and lie down so I can have a feel.'

They carried on chatting as Cat did so and she opened up her wrap-over dress.

'Ooh,' Gemma said as Cat's stomach danced away while she lay there. 'Someone's wide-awake.'

'I just grabbed a glass of orange juice,' Cat said. 'I think it's woken him up.'

Gemma examined her bump as they chatted and this evening she made an exception to their rule and was both doctor and friend.

'He's furious.' Cat sighed.

'Which makes two of you,' Gemma said. 'Ask him if he's told his wife yet! That might knock him off his high horse a touch…' Then she was kind. 'Cat, you had many reasons for not telling Dominic. Given all you've been through and Mike's reaction to the bad news, of course you're protective of this baby…'

'I just wanted to know it was okay before I said anything to Dominic.' Cat admitted what Gemma already had guessed. 'Then I wanted to get further along than I had with Thomas…' She closed her eyes for a moment because tears were on the verge of spilling out. Getting past twenty-five weeks had been a huge milestone. 'The last few weeks I've had no excuse, though.'

'So why didn't you tell him?'

'It was supposed to be a one-night stand. I don't want to discuss Thomas with a man I spent one night with. Do you know, I didn't even particularly like him? I thought he was a bit mean and dismissive.'

Gemma said nothing.

'Arrogant,' Cat said. 'Chauvinist… He wouldn't let me pay half for dinner.' She mimicked a deep voice. '"Why would you ruin a perfectly good night?" He's all the things I don't want in a man.'

Cat frowned as a blob of warm jelly was squirted onto her stomach. 'What are you doing?'

'An ultrasound.'

'I'm not due for one. Is there a problem?'

'No problem at all,' Gemma said, 'I just thought it might be nice for you to have a peek at your gorgeous baby. I'm recording it,' she added. 'Maybe Dominic might want to see it too.'

'Do you think?' Cat frowned. She loved having Gemma doing her ultrasounds—all her ultrasounds with Thomas had been fraught affairs. Mike had actually taken the probe out of the radiologist's hand once in an attempt to take over.

'I think that it might be a very nice olive branch,' Gemma said. 'It must be a shock for him and this might help him get used to the idea. When things get tense between the two of you, this might serve as a little re-minder that it's your baby you're discussing…'

Cat nodded and looked over at the screen.

It was a fun ultrasound. Gemma wasn't taking measurements, just a brief check that all was okay, which it was, and then they took a lovely long look.

There it was, opening its little mouth like a fish, and it was the most beautiful thing Cat had ever seen. 'What am I having?'

'You're sure you want to know?'

'I already know,' Cat said. 'I just want to hear it.'

'You're having a little girl,' Gemma said, and Cat felt as if the examination couch had dropped from beneath her, a little like turbulence on a plane.

'I was convinced it was a boy!'

'I know that you were,' Gemma said. 'She's beautiful. Look at those cheeks…'

It felt so different to look at the screen and to know it was her daughter that she was seeing. There she was, wiggling, waving and content in her own little world.

'Happy?' Gemma asked as Cat lay there.

Yes, she was dreading facing Dominic, yes, her life had been turned upside down and inside out but 'happy' was the right word.

Here, now, seeing her little girl, Cat was exactly that—happy.

'You're going to be a brilliant mum,' Gemma said, 'and, no matter how awkward things are between you and Dominic, I'm sure that you'll sort it out as best you can.'

After Cat had stood up and done up her dress, Gemma handed her the recording of the ultrasound and Cat put it in her bag.

'Good luck.' Gemma smiled.

'I'll need it.' She glanced at the clock. 'He's going to think I've stood him up.'

'He knows you've got an antenatal appointment?' Gemma checked, and Cat nodded. 'Well, surely he knows they don't run like clockwork…'

'Mike was always—'

'That was Mike,' Gemma said.

And this was Dominic.

'Hey, Cat,' Gemma said as she went to go. 'When you saw him again, did you still fancy him?'

'Moot point—I don't fancy married men.'

'Did you still fancy him?' Gemma persisted.

'Yes,' she admitted, 'but that's for this office only. The day I sit crying to my friend about whether or not I sleep with him because, of course, he and his wife never do it, or I start saying, he's going to leave his wife after Christmas…you have my permission to shoot me.'

'I shall and can you tell him from me that he's an utter bastard,' Gemma said.

'Oh, I shall.'

Trust Gemma to make her laugh, Cat thought as she walked the short distance to Oliver's. She was calmer than she'd expected to be as she stepped inside.

There was Dominic, sitting with a glass of wine and looking rather more rumpled than he had that morning. His tie was off, the top button of his shirt undone and his eyes were black with loathing as Cat made her way over.

She didn't expect him to stand for her.

Very deliberately he didn't.

It was a bit like walking into the headmaster's office, Cat thought, but refused to be rattled. She shook off her coat and put it on the low bench opposite him and then took a seat.

'Sorry, I'm a bit late. Gemma was running—'

'It's fine.'

Cat blinked at the ease of his acceptance.

It wasn't her timekeeping that was Dominic's concern!

'How was the appointment?'

'All's well,' Cat said.

'She's a good friend?' Dominic asked, and Cat nodded as she bristled in instant defence.

'Are you going to ask if that's wise?' she checked.

Dominic said nothing and she continued.

'Everybody seems to question whether or not I'm sensible to be seeing a friend, but—' Only then did he interrupt.

'You're a consultant and, from everything I heard at my interview and everything I've seen, you're meticulous and thorough, possibly a bit obsessive about certain details. I'm quite sure you've given your choice of obstetrician very careful thought. I'm sure your friend and you both discussed the pros and the cons of having her. I don't think there's anything I can add that you haven't already thought through.'

Cat felt the little bubble of indignation that she had around that topic deflate a touch.

'She's excellent.'

'I'm sure she is.'

'Have you heard from Andrew?' Cat asked.

'Nope,' Dominic said. 'I'm not really expecting to hear positive news. I'm quite sure you've had, or will be having, a quiet word in his ear...' He watched the colour mount on her cheeks as a waiter poured Cat some water and gave them menus. 'Though, if you haven't already, please think long and hard before you do. I assume you live close to work?'

'Sorry?'

'I'm just thinking for handovers and things.'

'Handovers?'

'Access visits, or whatever they're called.' Then he raised his voice just a fraction and the pink on her cheeks moved to a burning red. 'If we work at the same place, then it might make it a little easier when I want to spend time with *my* child!'

'I was going to tell you—' Cat attempted, but she didn't get very far.

'When it turned eighteen?' He shook his head. He clearly didn't believe her and she couldn't really blame him a bit for that. 'I don't think for a moment that you were going to tell me. In fact, I'm quite sure you'd already got what you needed from me that weekend.'

Cat's mouth gaped open. 'You think I deliberately got pregnant? What? That I'm some psycho going around pricking holes in condoms?' She shook her head and then met his eyes. 'I shouldn't be surprised. My mother thinks the same. Well, not quite that scenario but she seems to think I got bored one weekend and popped off to the sperm bank.' She dragged her eyes from his and looked at the menu as she spoke.

'I never set out to get pregnant.'

Dominic sat there and images of them making love danced before him—her hand rolling on a condom, another time, about to take her from behind, it had been Cat who had grabbed one and handed it to him.

If anything, it had been he who had been about to be careless, so ready had he been to take her.

It wasn't the best thought to be having right now and he reached for a wine and gave a small nod.

'Fair enough.

'And I did try to contact you. I spoke to some cheery woman in Glasgow who said that Dom had moved on…'

'It would have taken an hour tops to find me if you'd really wanted to,' he said.

'Have you told your wife yet?' She smirked as she read through the menu. 'Or were you hoping it wasn't yours?'

'Well, given my wife is all seeing and knowing now, I'd assume that she already knows.' He watched her frown. 'She's dead.'

Cat looked up.

'She's been dead for more than two years.'

'And you didn't think to tell me?'

'Don't even go there, Cat. You're the one keeping the big secret. Anyway, I *chose* not to tell you.'

'Why?'

'Because I didn't want *that* look.'

He didn't get to elaborate—the waiter was back and Cat ordered steak and a tomato salad and rolled her eyes because she really wanted seafood but it was on the list of noes that Gemma had given her. 'I'm never going to get my paella.'

'I'll have it for you,' he said, and ordered it.

'Bastard,' Cat said, even if she managed a small smile, but it soon faded as they got back to the serious talk once the waiter had gone.

'I didn't tell you at first because I wanted to make sure all the tests were okay…' The water she took a sip of seemed to burn as it went down. 'They were.'

'That's a poor excuse, Cat, because if they hadn't been

okay, a bit of notice that I'd be arranging my life around a special-needs child would have been appreciated.'

Again, his reaction surprised her. He didn't jump on results or demand facts. He had but one question.

'When's your due date?'

'The nineteenth of April.'

'Cat, I nearly bought a house in Spain last month. I was offered a job and that was going to be the starting date.'

'You can still take it,' Cat said, but rather quickly wished that she hadn't as his finger pointed in her direction and he shot out one word.

'Don't!'

He was doing his very best to stay level and calm but that she'd happily wave him off to Spain incensed him. 'I was pointing out how bloody late you've left it. I know!' Dominic said. 'How about you have the baby, I take it to Spain and you can see it during your annual leave?' He watched as her pink tongue bobbed out and she licked nervous lips. 'Yeah, not a nice thought, is it, Cat, so don't suggest the same for me. You need to get used to the idea that I'm not going to be some distant figure in my child's life. I'm going to be there, not just for Christmas and birthdays. I'm going to be doing the school pick-up and homework and I'll be there each and every parent-teacher night. You might not want me there and I fully get that we can't stand each other, so we can do it through lawyers if you prefer…'

'When did we get to not being able to stand each other?'

'Oh, about the time you started snooping through my wallet, about the time I found out that you'd deny me knowledge of my own child…'

'I thought you had a wife, maybe a family…'

'Even if I had, I still should have been told.'

Their food came then and she stared at his rather than hers.

'That was really horrible of me,' he admitted as he looked at his large plate of paella, especially as it looked seriously nice.

'Hopefully you'll have a massive allergic reaction.' Cat, less than sweetly, smiled.

'Yes, and no doubt you'll take ages to find the adrenaline pen so I'll be dead and that will take care of that…'

There was a tiny silence.

'When you said you didn't want to tell me you were a widower because of *that* look,' Cat said as she cut her steak. 'What did you mean?'

'Things change when you tell people that you're a widower…' He scooped out a mussel and then pulled a misty-eyed face that made her smile reluctantly. 'I can't really explain it. Honestly, since Heather died I've had more offers for sex than a rock star. Which sounds good but women seem to think I want to make love, or that I'm comparing them to my poor late wife, or even that I must want a wife… They don't get I just want to get down and dirty.'

'So we weren't making love?' Cat pouted and he smiled. 'Dominic, it was supposed to be a one-night stand.'

'And now we have to deal with the consequences.' He got back to his food. 'Did you find out what *we're* having?'

The 'we're' was very deliberate.

'I only just found that out now,' she said. 'A girl.'

She watched as his fork paused midway to his mouth and then he put it down.

The past ten days, since he had seen the maternity cover position being advertised, since he'd started to suspect she might be pregnant, had been spent in a whir of fury and concern. Now, in the midst of anger and change, he got a moment in the quiet centre of the storm.

A girl.

A daughter.

He just sat there as the news sank in and somehow, he had no idea how, it changed things, because, in that moment, he went from none to having not just one but two ladies to take care of and he looked at the bump of the little one and then into the eyes of her mum.

'Oh.'

'I know,' Cat said. 'I thought I was having a…' She was about to say *another boy* but she quickly changed. 'A boy.'

Yes, she understood Dominic a little better than he knew because she didn't want to be the recipient of *that* look.

Baby two after such a turbulent baby one was a private pain, one she could barely share with Gemma, let alone a man whose bed she'd been in for a single night.

No, he didn't need to know all about her.

There was a lot to talk about but they finished their meal in silence, lost in their own private thoughts.

'Have you thought of names?' Dominic asked as they put their cutlery down.

'I was leaning towards Harry till tonight.'

'I never thought I'd be running through baby names,' Dominic said.

'Didn't you and…?' She hesitated. It was none of her business whether or not he and his wife had planned on having children.

Dominic was grateful that she didn't finish the question. No, he and Heather hadn't got around to thinking of children. And he didn't want to share his wife with this virtual stranger.

'Do you want a quick coffee? Then I'm going to have to go,' he said, 'if I want to make my flight.'

'You're going back to Scotland tonight?'

'No, I'm going to Spain for a few days. As I said, I'm in the middle of relocating there and I've been looking at homes. Given that the baby is mine, there's a lot to do there. I'll have to withdraw my application and I'd like to do that in person, and I want to tell my parents face-to-face what's happening.'

'Will they be disappointed that you're not moving there now?'

'I don't think so. I wasn't exactly going to be living next door to them or anything. I expect they'll be surprised about the baby and then pleased.'

'Where are you flying out from?'

'Gatwick.'

'Good luck with your luggage,' Cat said, and gave a low laugh. 'I'll drive you.'

'I can take a taxi.'

'You're the one banging on about how we need to talk.'

He conceded with a nod.

'And no coffee for me, unfortunately.' Cat sighed. 'It gives me hiccoughs. I'm stuck with tea. I miss champagne, I miss coffee, I miss seafood…'

'I'll buy you the biggest bottle of champagne and have paella delivered to your hospital bed once the baby is here.'

It was a very nice thing to say, Cat thought. It was a nice thought to have because, even if they were the odd couple and doing this on the run, at least they weren't at each other's throats now.

'How did you find out about the baby?' Cat asked a little later as they walked to her car.

'Well, I keep an eye on jobs and things and I saw one come up in your department. I remembered something you said about being the only female consultant…'

She flashed the lights of her car and they walked over to it.

'I told myself that I was being ridiculous. You could have been married or anything…'

'Would you have cared if I was married that weekend?' she asked.

'No,' he admitted.

'I don't like you,' Cat said, but he just laughed.

'You don't have to like me. Anyway, I'd never have cheated on my wife, but that weekend, had you been cheating…' Dominic shrugged. 'Anyway, it's all hypothetical.'

'But very telling.'

'Do you want me to lie to you, Cat, just say the right thing?'

'No.'

'Anyway, back to how I tracked you down—the dates for the leave all added up and…' They stopped talking as they got in but once they were pulling out of the car park the conversation resumed. 'I was going to call you but then I decided to surprise you.'

'That wasn't very nice.'

'No, I know that it wasn't,' he said. 'I wasn't feeling very nice at the time, but...' He didn't continue, they just drove in silence, but as the airport came into view conversation started again. 'You haven't chosen badly, Cat. I might have been a bit of a bastard the way I landed on you and some of the things I've said tonight but I'm not going to be a negative in your baby's life. And,' he added, 'I'm sure you don't need my opinion of you but when I think of some of the women that I could have been having this conversation with, I'm very happy that it's you. I think you'll be a brilliant mum and I'm quite sure we'll do this right. We've still got a couple of months to work things out...'

'We do,' Cat said.

He went into his wallet, pulled out a business card and wrote a few things on the back and Cat frowned when she read them.

'Why would I need your social network details? I'm not going to be checking up on you...' Then she went pink when she recalled how he'd caught her going through his wallet.

'Or me you,' Dominic said. 'But if you update about the baby and things...'

'I'll call you if there's a problem.'

'I meant for day-to-day stuff,' he said. 'I don't need formal emails and progress updates. Soon you might want the same...'

'Sorry?'

'Well, she won't stay a baby. My family lives in Spain.'

'You'd take her on holiday? No.'

She was adamant, her response was instant. 'You're not taking her out of the country.'

And Dominic was about to respond that his lawyer would see to it but he held that in. He could see the conflict in her eyes and he knew that she was struggling with the concept.

Cat was. She had glimpsed the future.

There would be pictures of her child with her father in houses she never set foot in. Holidays spent apart.

'I just sent a friend request,' Dominic said. 'Up to you whether or not you accept it.'

'Here...' She went into her bag and wrote down her number, then she remembered the recording.

'What's this?'

'I had an ultrasound today. If you want to see her...'

'Thanks.'

He went to get out of the car. 'I am sorry for not telling you, Dominic.'

He gave her a grim smile. 'Yeah, well, I don't accept your apology—I'm not that magnanimous. Call me when you need to...'

'I shan't.'

'Oh, I'm sure you'll have questions.'

'I won't.'

But even before she got home Cat had found several.

Would he want to be at the birth?

The very thought filled her with horror!

Cat did her best to stay in control and the one place she was guaranteed to lose it was in the labour ward.

No, she did not want arrogant, surly Dominic seeing her swearing like a sailor and breaking down.

No way!

And what were they going to tell people at work?

Her mind was darting as she stepped back into her home.

She put some washing on and, completely wrecked from a long and difficult day, wrestled off her boots, which was very hard with a stomach like a basketball, and then had a very quick bath and went to bed.

Except, though tired, she couldn't sleep and she picked up her phone and, sure enough, there was his friend request, which she accepted.

His status was given as single and Cat frowned, wondering why he didn't say he was widowed.

Oh, that's right, he loathed *that* look.

Then she smiled when she read his status. A little cryptic note that she was sure was aimed at her.

You can run but you can't hide.

She carried on reading and looking at photos of his eccentric parents and terribly beautiful sister and then there she was.

Heather.

She knew it was her from the photo she had glimpsed in the hotel.

Now she felt as if she was snooping, so she went back to Dominic and saw a picture of him all wet and gorgeous coming out of a swimming pool. At thirty weeks pregnant and not wanting to be, she was terribly, terribly turned on.

'So not happening,' she said, and turned off her phone.

His body was still there, goading her to have another glimpse, at six the next morning when she drank her tea and switched her phone back on.

But then she smiled when she saw what he had changed his relationship status to.

It's complicated.

It most certainly was but, the funniest thing was that as she dressed for work and headed out to face the day, even if they weren't together, they were on the same side—her baby had a father and that sat right with Cat.

She didn't feel quite so alone.

CHAPTER SEVEN

DOMINIC'S PARENTS WERE, though initially surprised, completely delighted with the news.

There was too much wine drunk and they spoke late into the night, and they kept making the most ridiculous suggestions.

'Why don't you bring her here so we can get to know her and she can have a little holiday?'

'She's thirty weeks pregnant,' Dominic said, and looked over at Kelly for some help.

'Mum, they're not a couple,' his sister said.

'Perhaps, but I'd still like to meet her. We could come over.' His mother, Anna, was warming to the idea. 'We could fly over for the birth. I'd love to see my granddaughter being born.'

Dominic swore under his breath before answering. 'I don't even know if I'm going to be present at the birth...'

'You could film it,' Anna said. 'Live-stream it.'

'And then you could set it to music and forward it to your hippy friends...' Dominic sarcastically responded, and when his father nodded this time Dominic swore out loud. 'You weren't even there when we...' he gestured to Kelly '...were born.'

'And I regret it to this day,' James said. 'That's the beauty of being a grandparent, you get to do things right the second time around.'

What planet were they from? Dominic wondered.

Even if they made him laugh, they drove him mad at times, and this was one of those times. He could only imagine how well that suggestion would go down with the cool and rather distant Cat.

Yes, they made him laugh, because he was doing that now as he pictured her shocked expression as he told her he wanted to film the birth.

'Cat and I are going to sort things out between us.' Dominic told his parents how it would be. 'Preferably without lawyers. You guys need to stay back.'

'From our grandchild?'

He closed his eyes for a brief moment. He'd never considered having a baby but now that he was he wanted his parents in his child's life, so he thought long and hard before answering.

'From Cat and me,' he said. 'We've got two months to work things out. You're to stay out of things.'

Anna didn't answer. In fact, Dominic was sure she shook her head.

After his parents had gone to bed, he sat, listening to the trickle from the pool filter and enjoying sitting with his sister outside. It was cool and they had the gas heaters on but after a cold Scottish winter it was blissful.

'I love it here,' Dominic said.

'Would Cat?'

'Oh, we are so far from that, Kelly,' he said. 'It was a one-night stand, a weekend conference...'

'That's completely changed your life,' Kelly said. 'You were all set to move here.'

'I was *almost* all set,' he said.

'Almost?'

'I don't want to talk about it.'

He didn't.

He didn't want to tell his sister that, despite the seriousness of his plans, since August they had started to change. Unable to get that night out of his mind, and furious at how the weekend had ended, he had considered calling Cat to explain things. And if he was thinking about calling her, it had seemed a bit nonsensical to be considering moving further away than he was already.

Yes, he hadn't been idly flicking through jobs in London.

He'd been wondering how he could ask her to give them a chance.

'Is there any hope for the two of you?' Kelly asked. 'You obviously fancied each other and you said things went well when you saw her again…'

'Kelly, the stakes are a lot higher now. Surely we should be concentrating on how we're best going to be as parents rather than trying to establish a relationship.'

'I guess.'

'What if it doesn't work? What if we give it a go and one of us wants to end it? God, we don't need hurt feelings and resentment added to the mix. I hardly know anything about her.'

'Does she know about Heather?'

'I told her tonight that I was a widower.'

'Tonight?' Kelly checked.

'Yep.'

'So what were you two talking about that weekend?'

Dominic rolled his eyes. 'We weren't really talking.'

Except that wasn't entirely true.

They had talked, they had shared more than sex. That was the reason he had wanted to look her up.

'I took her to Collserola Park,' Dominic said. 'We watched the sun come up. You know how Heather had a thing about sunrise?' he asked, and Kelly nodded. 'Not once, when I've been with someone, have I felt guilty. It's always just been sex and I knew Heather would get that but that morning, sitting watching the sun come up with someone who wasn't Heather, was the most unfaithful I'd ever felt.'

'It sounds like you two have something to build on...'

'Maybe,' he said. 'But it would be foolish at best to rush this. I've had one brilliant marriage, Kelly. I'm not downgrading for the second one. Right now Cat and I need to sort out how we're going to be for the baby. The two of us as a couple will just have to wait. I'm not going to see her for another three weeks and that's if I even get the job.'

'Won't she see to it that you do?'

Dominic managed a wry laugh. 'You have a far sweeter mind than I do, or Cat come to that. I'm quite sure she'll be seeing to it that I don't.'

They said goodnight and as he lay in bed he took out his laptop and plugged in the recording and saw for the first time the life they had made.

She was beautiful, so beautiful that it actually brought tears to his eyes.

It should feel like a mistake—surely this was something he should have been doing with Heather—and yet, seeing his baby on the screen, thinking of Cat...

It didn't feel like a mistake.

It felt right.

Was there a chance for them?

Could strangers who had shared just a night have got it so right that they could spend the rest of their lives together?

Cautious with his emotions, it had taken years to get around to getting engaged to Heather.

They had gone out for more than two years before they'd moved in together.

Another three years before they'd got married.

And they hadn't been ready to even start trying for a baby before Heather had been taken ill.

He flicked on his social media site and saw that Cat had accepted his friend request and it was Dominic who snooped.

She had the most boring page ever.

He found out nothing new about her, other than that her star sign was Virgo and that her friends wrote on her wall more than she did.

No mention of Spain, no lovers' names.

Nothing.

He wanted to know more, though, and even if they needed to be concentrating on the baby, somehow they had to make time for them, and that was why he changed his status.

Not single.

Not in a relationship.

It's complicated sounded about right, so that, for now, would do.

CHAPTER EIGHT

'YOU SOUND OUT of breath,' Dominic commented.

It was Thursday night, a few days since they'd met, and Cat had only just arrived home when she answered her phone and it was him.

'That's because I just took my boots off.' She sighed. 'Which is no mean feat these days.'

'I'm just calling to let you know what you probably do already—Andrew called this afternoon while I was flying back from Spain and left a cheery message, asking me to call him. So it sounds like I got the job.'

'You did,' Cat said, flicking on the kettle.

'Do you have an issue with that?'

'I did,' she admitted, 'but I don't now.'

'He's also asked if I can start a couple of weeks before I officially take up your position. Do you have an issue with that?'

'A bit,' she admitted, 'but I'll get over it. How was Spain?'

'Still beautiful.'

'How were your parents with the news?'

'Elated.'

'Oh!'

'Invasive.'

'Okay.' She let out a laugh. 'It's not just them. Honestly, people think they can ask me the most personal questions and as for touching my bump...' She shuddered.

'I promise not to touch your bump uninvited.'

'Thank you.'

'I'm coming down this weekend and I'll be looking at houses. I'm just checking you're not planning on moving in the near future...'

Cat was silent. He really had meant it when he'd said he wanted to be around for his child.

'No, I have no plans to move. Well, I might need a bigger house but I shan't be leaving the area.' She thought for a moment. 'You're not going to move too close, though? I mean...'

'I don't want to be your neighbour, Cat. Just close enough to make things easier on both of us. I was going to rent but I've been doing that for a couple of years. I want to give her a proper base.'

'Sounds good. While I've got you on the phone I actually do have a couple of questions,' she said.

She had quite a list actually.

'Can they keep till the weekend?' he asked. 'I'm a bit swamped right now.'

'Sure.'

'We can go out for dinner and discuss things.'

And if he could be so brusque and direct, without apology, then so too could she.

'I don't want to go out,' she said, because she'd had to swap to get this weekend off and there was a lot to be done. By evening all she would be ready for was a night flopped on the sofa. 'I don't want to discuss my private life in a restaurant. You can come here.'

'Okay, don't worry about cooking, though.'

'Oh, I shan't.'

'Saturday, about six?' Dominic checked. 'I'll come when I've finished looking through houses.'

'Whenever,' Cat said.

She heard a voice in the background.

A female voice.

'I have to go.'

He was probably at work, she told herself as she ended the call.

And even if he wasn't, it was none of her business.

Cat really didn't have time to dwell on her feelings, if she even had feelings for Dominic. Aware she was only going to get bigger and that there weren't too many days off between now and her maternity leave starting, when Saturday came she found herself back in the wallpaper shop. This time she had Gemma in tow and her brother's offer to come and help this afternoon when the cot was being delivered.

'We have the softest pink,' Veronica said. 'It actually feels like candy floss…'

'The last time I ate candy floss I vomited,' Cat said to Gemma.

'It's gorgeous,' Gemma insisted as she ran her hands over it, but Cat shook her head as she opened up another sample book.

'That,' Cat said, 'is what I call gorgeous.'

'It's blue!'

It was *so* blue, the paper was every shade of night and brushed with dandelions that looked as if they could blow away in the night wind.

And so Cat found herself up a ladder as her brother, Greg, hovered nervously. He had no idea how to hang wallpaper so he held the ladder instead and handed her the glued sheets to put up.

'It's very dark,' Greg offered, when she was done.

'It's supposed to be for sleeping,' Cat said. 'You don't like it?'

'I don't know,' Greg admitted. 'Maybe when the cot's in and you've got the right furniture and light fittings...'

'You have no imagination, Greg.'

'I'm an accountant,' Greg said. 'What time's the cot arriving?'

'It's a p.m. delivery, that's all they'd say.' A knock at the door had Cat smiling. 'You can help set it up while I go and get changed.'

'Help?'

Cat laughed as Greg went down to get the door and then she looked around the bedroom. 'A brave choice' had been Veronica's words when she had made her selection. Gemma had looked worried and Greg was sitting on the fence...

'Cat!' Greg called. 'The cot's here and so is the reason for its purchase.'

Dominic gave a wry grin as Cat's brother announced his early arrival.

He had surprised himself with his own reaction when he had seen a man waiting for the delivery of the cot.

A good-looking man around Cat's age.

It had taken only a moment to work out it was probably her brother, and as he introduced himself the same green eyes had confirmed that fact.

Dominic, though, was unsettled by his brief two-bulls-in-one-paddock moment.

Another thing that needed to be discussed, he thought.

No, he wasn't particularly looking forward to tonight.

Then he changed his mind because, wearing khaki trousers and with a vest top on, Cat came down the stairs and he noticed that between now and earlier this week her belly button had poked out.

'Dominic.' Cat gave a wary smile at the strange air of hostility in her hallway. 'This is my brother, Greg.'

'We've already introduced ourselves,' Greg said as the delivery man dragged cardboard boxes up her stairs. 'Right, I'm off.' Greg gave his sister a brief kiss on the cheek.

'I thought you were going to stay and help with the cot.'

'Er...Cat,' Greg said, 'I'm sure Dominic can manage that much at least...so long as it's not too much responsibility for him...'

Oh, no!

She groaned inwardly as Greg got all big brother and angry and tried to somehow equate putting up a cot with men who impregnated helpless virgins and left them heavy with child.

'I've got this, thanks, Greg,' she said, but only as her brother shot Dominic a filthy look and then stalked off did it dawn on her what the problem was.

'Oh, God,' she said to Dominic. 'I forgot to tell him you weren't married.'

'Remind me never to take over a multi-trauma patient from you,' he said.

'What?'

'Well, you're not very good at passing on pertinent information.' He smiled. 'Anyway, the mood he's in, it wouldn't have made a difference. I'm still the one-night stand who left his precious little sister pregnant.'

'He hasn't been like that...' she was about to say,

since she'd broken down on Greg about Mike, but now wasn't the time and anyway she had to sign for the delivery, so she finished with a lame '…in ages.'

He waited till she'd signed for the cot and the door was closed before he continued speaking.

'Well, next time you're talking, if you could slip into the conversation that I'm not cheating on my wife, it would be appreciated.'

'I shall.'

Dominic doubted it.

He assumed he was way down on her list of topics of conversation.

He assumed rightly.

But he was up at the top of her thoughts.

Inappropriate thoughts for a heavily pregnant woman about a man she didn't particularly like.

'Lovely hallway,' he said.

'Come through.' She opened the door to the lounge and Dominic stood there for a moment.

'This is such a sight for sore eyes after some of the dumps I've seen today.'

'Did you find anything you liked?'

'One that I liked.' He told her the address and it was close but not too close. 'It needs far too much work, though.'

'Ooh,' Cat said. 'Tell me.'

And so he told her about the dodgy plumbing, the ancient kitchen, fireplaces, cornices and the disgusting bathroom with green carpet and a study that was completely covered in cork tiles.

'That sounds like my idea of heaven,' Cat said, and she went to her perfect mantelpiece and took down a photo. 'This was what this room looked like when I bought the place.'

'Oh, my God, it's worse than the one I saw today.'

'We can do a tour if you like,' she said. 'I love showing off my handiwork.'

'You renovated it?'

'Every last bit of it.'

'Oh, my…' he said as they walked down her hallway and to the kitchen. 'We could swap houses,' he said. 'You could renovate mine while you're on maternity leave…'

'I might be a bit busy, Dominic,' she said.

'I'm sure you could fit it in,' he teased, and yet it made Cat smile because everyone else told her how zoned out and incapable she was going to be once the baby was here.

He seemed to know her better than everyone else.

It was strange, it was nice.

It was unexpected.

She took down a picture from the fridge and showed Dominic the absolute disaster the kitchen had once been.

'I didn't have a sink for the first three months. I had to do my dishes in the purple room of pain upstairs.'

'Show me your purple room of pain, Cat…'

Whoops, were they flirting?

Up the stairway they went, admiring the wooden bannister as they did so. 'There were about twenty layers of gloss paint,' Cat told him, and then she opened the bathroom door and took a photo from a small dark wooden chest so he might understand just how painful purple could be.

'Everything was purple,' Cat said, 'even the toilet seat cover…'

'But it's like something you'd find at a yoga retreat now,' he said. 'Not that I frequent them, but if I did...' he looked at the rolled white towels on the dark wood and the gorgeous claw-foot bath '...well, I'd demand a bathroom like this.'

'It's fabulous, isn't it?' she said. 'But the place is tiny. No room for a nanny.'

'A nanny?'

'I'm going to be working full-time, Dominic.' She didn't look to see his expression. 'Do you want to see her room?'

'The nanny's?'

'The baby's.'

'I would.'

She was a little nervous about opening the door, she wasn't sure why, but as she did and he stepped in, she found she was holding her breath. Dominic looked around.

'It's like...' he started, and she braced herself for 'a brave choice' or to be told how dark it was, or for Dominic to point out that it was dark blue when they were having a little girl. 'It's like a magical night-time,' Dominic said. 'It's amazing. You just want to...'

'Say it!'

'Sleep!'

'Yes.' Cat was delighted. 'That's what I thought. It's just so dark and peaceful and once the curtains are in and the light fittings...'

'And the cot,' he said, looking at it all piled against the wall. 'Do I have to do that?'

'You'd look a right bastard if you left it for me to do.'

'Fair call,' Dominic said. 'Right, shall I go and get dinner?'

Cat nodded.

'Anything in particular?'

'I'd love a hot curry,' she said. 'And mango chutney…'

'How hot?'

'Very hot.'

'Okay.' Dominic frowned. 'But I thought pregnant women would avoid curries…'

'What's the population of India?' Cat asked as they walked back down the hall. 'I'd like a beef curry and lots of naan. You get dinner and I'm going to have a bath and get changed.'

'What's in there?' Dominic asked, fully knowing they were passing her bedroom door.

'Something you'll never see.' She smirked as he headed off.

But as Dominic got into the car and Cat stripped for the bath, she wondered if she should just run it cold to put out the fire down below. They'd both known she was lying.

Her bedroom was *yet* to be seen.

Which was a problem.

A very real one.

Sex would only make things complicated.

And they were complicated enough already.

CHAPTER NINE

HE WAS GONE for ages.

Ages.

So much so that when Cat came out of the bath and peered out of her bedroom window and saw that there was no car coming down the street, instead of quickly dressing, she took a few minutes to put on moisturiser. As she rubbed it into her stomach she wondered just how much bigger she could get.

She put on a long grey tube dress and then combed through her hair.

Still no car.

Was he shopping for ingredients? she wondered.

She didn't bother with make-up.

Instead, she poured a nice big glass of iced water, her latest favourite drink, and then she put the door on the latch and went back upstairs and started taking the cardboard off the cot.

'It's open,' she called, when he finally arrived. 'I'll be down soon.'

Dominic was serving up dinner when she came down five or so minutes later, carrying a pile of cardboard.

'Come and eat.'

She did so, but first she poured herself a small glass

of antacid for her inevitable heartburn and he smiled as she took a seat on the floor at the coffee table, where he had set up.

'If I'm going to get heartburn, I want it to be worth it,' she said. 'It smells fantastic. Where did you go?'

'About fifteen minutes away. I worked near here a few years ago and I was guessing this curry house wouldn't have closed down.'

She could see why it hadn't when she tasted the curry.

'We can put the cot up after dinner,' he suggested, and Cat nodded.

'It will be good to have that room done.'

'You had some questions for me.'

'I do,' she agreed, and took a breath. 'Are you going to tell people at work that, well, that you're going to be a father?'

'I don't know.'

'And if you do, are you going to say that the mother is me?'

Dominic pondered for a moment. He hadn't thought this through properly. 'I guess not. Well, not at first. Maybe once you've gone on leave, or you've had the baby. Has anyone actually asked who the father is?'

'Not at work,' Cat said. 'Well, not directly. I keep my personal life to myself pretty much.'

'Okay,' he said. 'Well, you don't have to worry about me saying anything. What else?'

She was rather nervous to ask the next one. 'Are you going to want to be there at the birth?'

This question Dominic had thought about. 'I think that depends on what you want, and I would guess that you might not want me there...' He gave a tight shrug and then he looked at Cat for her response.

'I don't want to rob you of anything, but...'

'Just the first six months of the pregnancy,' he sniped, and then he stopped trying to score points. 'Sorry, go on.'

She didn't really know how best to say it. 'If you add it all up, we've probably spent less than forty-eight hours together.'

'I get that.'

'And I just think I'd do better on my own.'

'Fair enough.'

She was grateful for his words but she knew that it wasn't completely fine with him, that she was denying him being present at the birth of his daughter.

Well, tough, she thought, scooping some curry onto her naan. Surely some things were better unseen!

'My parents both want to be there, though,' Dominic said suddenly, and she nearly choked on the water she was drinking. She looked at his expressionless face and she had no idea if he was joking. 'I pointed out that I didn't even know whether I'd be there and they suggested that you film it...'

'For them?' she croaked, and he nodded. 'I know we don't know each other very well,' she said, 'but I trust we know each other enough that you said an emphatic no.'

'I did,' he said. 'While I wouldn't normally presume to speak on your behalf I delivered that no for you and reminded my father that he was away on business when I was born and didn't see me till I was six weeks old.'

'Really?'

'This apple fell very far from that tree. I'll be seeing her very soon after she's born.'

'Of course.'

He got up then and Cat waited as he went out to the car and when he came back he handed her a bag. 'I wasn't going to give this to you.'

'What is it?'

'My mother's been shopping.'

She most certainly had. Wow, the Spanish had amazing taste in baby clothes. There were tiny little sleepsuits and little hats and cute socks and a thick envelope, which Cat opened with a frown.

'I've no idea…' Dominic said.

'They just wanted to say congratulations,' she said as she read the letter, 'and to let me know that whatever goes on between us two, I'm welcome any time in their home.'

'Too much?' he checked.

'No,' she admitted. 'That's actually very nice of them.' She thought for a moment—it really was. Suddenly her baby had a whole other family and, aside from Dominic, they included her.

'Don't expect the same from my family,' Cat warned.

'Oh, I don't.' Dominic smiled. 'Next question.'

'I'm hoping to breastfeed. I know that you'll want to see her and have her stay over, but…'

'Not till she's old enough,' he said. 'I understand that she'll need her mum. Maybe we play that one by ear, trust that we'll work out what's right for her.'

'Okay.'

It sounded a lot better than trying to work out some neat arrangement with a lawyer.

'Any more questions?'

'I think that's it,' she said. She'd had loads but, really, now that he'd said they'd play things by ear she felt soothed by that.

'You're sure?' he said, as if he expected there to be more, but Cat nodded.

'Do you?' she asked.

'Well, I guess that I do… Are you seeing anyone at the moment? I mean, is there someone who's going to…?' He couldn't really admit that he didn't like the idea of another man being more of a constant in his child's life than he was but Cat had started to laugh.

'I have no idea why, Dominic,' she said, 'but I can't seem to pull lately. It's like I've got two heads or something.' Then she was serious. 'No, I'm not seeing anyone.'

It didn't fully answer the sudden questions that filled both their minds, how they'd feel about the other dating, but they decided to drop that hot coal for now.

After dinner they headed upstairs and between them they put up the cot.

'This is about as far as my DIY skills go,' Dominic warned. 'I only know how to use a drill from my orthopaedic rotation.'

It was more a fiddly job than a difficult one, though it was easier with two, but after a few attempts it was up. Cat put in the mattress and then Dominic checked that the side slid up and down.

'Do you think,' Dominic asked as they surveyed their handiwork, 'that I should maybe get the same wallpaper for her room at my place?'

'I think that would be really nice for her.'

For the first time she glimpsed the two of them getting this right, not just able to manage but that their daughter's future would be better for having him in her life.

'I'm sorry I didn't let you know,' she said. 'I had my reasons.'

'You thought I was married,' he said. 'I really wish you hadn't gone snooping that day. I don't like snoops.'

'I don't usually. Remember on the beach, when I went to get the mouthguard?'

He frowned in recall as Cat spoke on.

'I saw a ridge in your wallet that felt like a ring and then I kept seeing a pink line on your ring finger, and the more you stayed out in the sun the pinker it got. When you were having a shower I let curiosity get the better of me.'

'Fair enough,' he said. 'I'd only just started to take the ring off.'

'Why didn't you tell me you were widowed?'

'I wasn't ready to share her with you,' Dominic said. 'That might sound odd…'

'No, no, I get it.'

That part Cat did, because she still wasn't ready to share Thomas.

'Heather had several brain tumours and that's all I want to say about it.'

'Okay,' she said, and she glanced over and saw how uncomfortable he was with the topic. 'We didn't sign up for this, did we?'

He understood what she was trying to say. 'The baby's actually the easy part.'

It was opening up and sharing your life with another person that was the difficult bit.

He looked down at her stomach and the mini-gymnast within, because in her tight dress you could see the baby moving. Cat did the right thing.

She took his hand and he felt the solid bulge of their child's head trying to climb into Cat's ribs, and then she guided his hand down past her belly button to a foot, and then she left him free to roam.

And that lump of hot coal that they had dodged was back, it had to be, because she was terribly hot and for once it had nothing to do with the extra person she was carrying.

It had more to do with the reason her baby was there.

'Haven't you got another question, Cat?'

Her cheeks were pink and she wondered how to broach the most difficult question of all.

'Us.' Dominic did it for her. 'Dating.'

She swallowed.

'My parents and sister all seem to think we should give us a go,' he said. 'I've told them that it's the most terrible idea I've ever heard.'

'Terrible?'

'Well, we know the sex part would be fine...'

'You assume it would be fine,' Cat corrected.

'I know it would be fine for me,' he said. 'I've never found a pregnant woman attractive till now...' His hand was on her stomach and it wanted to move up to the thick nipple and stroke it, he wanted that dress off, and from the loaded silence between them he guessed that she did too. 'From my perspective,' he said with a low, sexy huskiness, 'I'd have no problem doing you on the floor right now.'

'You could,' she admitted.

'But then what?' He looked at her and met eyes that glittered with lust. 'What if we break up? What if it doesn't work out between us?'

'I don't know.'

'So,' he said, when he'd far rather not, 'no sex for

us, none of the easy part. What I'm proposing is six months…'

'Of what?'

'No dating anyone else…just us, getting to know each other, working out how we can be friends, concentrating on the baby…'

It was the most sensible thing she had ever heard.

She should be cheering really.

No pressure, no stepping on the roller-coaster, no promises made that might prove impossible to keep.

No sex.

It was the last part she was wrestling with.

'Sure.' She smiled. 'Can you remove your hand, please?'

'Yep.' He did so. 'I'm going to go,' he said.

'Where are you staying?'

He didn't answer her question. 'I start work in three weeks on Monday…'

'Where will you stay? I mean, even if you put in an offer on the house…'

'Not your problem, Cat,' he said, though he said it nicely. 'You worry about yourself and the baby. I'll sort out things at my end.'

He did.

The next day he had another look at the house before heading for home. It was a ten-minute walk from Cat's.

Two weeks later, driving home, Cat found herself slowing the car down as she always did when she drove past it.

Actually, she had no need at all to be driving past.

She just did these days.

SOLD.

She tried to imagine the future.

Stopping the car at this very spot and getting her baby and its bags out and handing her heart over to him.

She couldn't.

And it was even harder to imagine driving off.

Going home alone to an empty house when the people she loved were in another one.

No, Cat corrected, the baby she loved...

No, a little voice told her, *you are crazy about him and have been since the moment you met him.*

They just didn't know each other at all.

CHAPTER TEN

THERE WASN'T REALLY the chance to get to know each other.

Cat's pregnancy continued to gallop along at breakneck speed and for Dominic, seeing the bank, sorting out the purchase of his house, working his notice and arranging to move his stuff to England had his blood boiling about how hard Cat had made it by not telling him.

Then he'd remember the reason he was moving his life several hundred miles and *not* in the planned direction of Spain and he chose to let it go.

He didn't move in on the weekend before he started working at the Royal. Cat knew that because, after a long weekend on call, she drove home on the Monday morning and the house was still untouched.

And even if their paths didn't cross during those first few days at work she certainly knew that he had started because she heard the nurses discussing the sexy new doctor.

'Is he seeing someone?' Cat heard Marcia asking Julia on their coffee break early one evening. 'He doesn't have a ring.'

'I don't know,' Julia said. 'I'm going to ask him when

he comes on.' She smiled at Cat, who was taking a seat. 'How many weeks now?'

'Thirty-four,' Cat said.

'When do you finish up?' Marcia asked.

'Just next week to go.'

If she lasted that long.

She ached, her stomach was huge and she felt as if she was wearing some awful fake pregnancy outfit. She was all boobs and belly and even though it was cold and just coming into spring, she was permanently too hot and felt as if she was wrapped in a blanket.

She was dressed in her grey tube dress with her hair worn up just to keep it off her neck and a small cotton cardigan to stop people asking her if she was cold. 'You're on nights next week, aren't you?' Julia groaned in sympathy. 'I am too. I can wheel you around in one of the wheelchairs.'

Cat smiled. 'I might just take you up on that!'

They'd all tried to subtly prise out of her who the father was but had accepted that she didn't want to tell. Apart from that, though, she was getting on better with everyone. Yes, she was more than back to her old, pre-Mike self.

Cat was sipping on iced water and trying not to fan herself when Dominic walked in and Marcia and Julia perked up.

'How's the move?' Julia asked.

'Not happening till the weekend,' Dominic said, and took a seat and nodded to Cat.

'Are you on tonight?' Cat checked, and glanced at the clock. It was only seven and he wasn't due to start till nine.

'I am. I'm here now if you want to finish up.'

Cat shot him a warning look. She did not need him babysitting her and so she said nothing.

She didn't need to; Julia took care of that.

'So, is it just you moving in?' she fished. 'Or have your whole family relocated?'

'Just me,' Dominic said.

'So you're not married?'

'No.'

'Girlfriend?' Marcia asked.

'Nope.'

'So you're single!' Julia beamed.

She wasn't smiling for long.

'Julia?' Dominic asked. 'Why would you assume that just because I haven't got a girlfriend that I'm not in a relationship?'

She watched Julia frown as she tried to work it out and Dominic got up and left.

'Does that mean he's gay?' Marcia asked. 'Does that mean…?'

Cat left them to it but she did have to smother her smile as she tapped him on the shoulder in the kitchen. 'Don't start coming in early so you can cover for me. If I need help…'

'Oh, for God's sake,' he said. 'I'm staying with friends at the moment and they've got three children all under five. Believe me, I would far rather be at work.'

'Oh.'

'So stay if you want to, go home if you like…'

She stayed, but it was only on principle.

By 8:00 p.m. the department was quiet and the few patients they had were all either waiting to go to the ward or waiting for their lab work to come back.

'So you're moving at the weekend?' she asked.

'Yep.' Dominic rolled his eyes. 'I knew I was buying a bomb but when I got the keys... You should see it.'

She'd like to see it. Only, he didn't offer.

The only solace she had was the exclusion zone he'd put around dating, so she knew he wasn't busy with someone else.

She just sensed his dark mood.

'I'm going home,' she said.

''Night.'

Yes, his mood was dark.

It was two years to the day since Heather had died.

Last year at this time he had realised he had to move on.

He'd just never expected his life to head in this direction, and moving in at the weekend was going to be hell.

It was.

All the furniture he'd had brought down proved to be an expensive mistake, because it ended up being donated. He watched the charity truck drive off with half of his life on board and as he took delivery of a cot he felt as if he were on Pluto.

He was back in London minus a wife.

And about to become a father by a woman he barely knew.

It was time to rectify that.

Cat came in from work on Sunday evening and there was a note on her door, inviting her to dinner.

She stopped at the supermarket and bought flowers, which was very back to front, but, then, every part of them was back to front. Seeing her standing there, holding a bunch of daffodils, made him smile when he opened the door.

'I was lying to Marcia and Julia. I'm not gay.'

'Yes, well, I'd worked that one out. You can still like flowers, though.'

Spring had sprung and he looked in a box to find a glass because he didn't own a suitable vase.

He chose not to explain that he had once owned a heavy crystal vase that had been a wedding present but he'd got rid of it and there was a little hand-blown glass one they'd bought on their honeymoon. He couldn't bear to part with it or put Cat's flowers in it.

Then he chose to open up a little.

'It was Heather's two-year anniversary the other day...'

'I'm sorry.'

'And I've just got rid of a truckload of our stuff. Not everything, but...' Yes, he was bad at sharing and so the daffodils got a beer mug, which felt a whole lot better than placing them in *their* vase.

She knew there was nothing she could say and Dominic was very glad that she didn't try.

'Do you want a tour?' he offered.

'I thought you'd never ask.'

He saw disaster, Cat saw potential.

'This house is going to be amazing,' she said as she walked through.

'It smells,' Dominic said. 'It didn't the last time I walked through it.'

'They'd have sprayed something.' Cat laughed. 'You've got damp...'

He knew that from the surveyor's report.

'Not much, though,' she said. 'And you could just get rid of this wall...'

'Sure you don't want to swap houses?'

'I'm very sure.' She smiled. 'I've got enough to do

at mine. I think I'm nesting. I keep washing things and folding things—it's really disconcerting.'

'Here.' He opened up a cupboard and pulled out a jumble of laundry. 'If you feel the need.'

'I shan't.'

Dinner was nice.

A lovely lamb roast he had made, better than the frozen meal Cat would have managed before falling into bed.

'I start nights tomorrow,' she said. 'Four of them, and then I'm out of that place.'

'Are you looking forward to stopping work?'

'Now I am,' she admitted. 'At first I wanted to work right up to the last minute but not now.'

She was now thirty-five weeks, soon to be thirty-six, and the thought of four weeks or more of this was daunting, to say the least.

'I got a cot,' Dominic said.

'I saw.'

'I'm quite sure you don't want to put up another one...'

Actually, she did.

'I know she won't be here much at first, but if she is, it's better she has somewhere she can sleep,' Dominic said. 'I'll get around to decorating it...' He looked at the woman who wasn't the woman he was supposed to have been doing this with and then he looked away.

'I'm really sorry you're hurting,' she said.

'It's not your fault. It just is what it is. Tomorrow's the anniversary of her funeral. There are just all these bloody dates in March...'

July was her horrible month.

This one would be as hard as the first for she'd be

telling Thomas that he was a big brother now. She'd be at her happiest and saddest at the very same time and she didn't quite know how she'd deal with it.

And, yes, perhaps then she could have told him but she found it impossible to share that most painful part of herself.

She didn't trust his reaction.

The death of a child was agony.

The death of a child, when it was suggested by the people you love most, even her own parents, that it might be a blessing, made it a place you chose not to go with others.

One wrong word from Dominic, she knew, would kill her inside.

'I'm going to go,' Cat said, because they were too new to be too close. 'Give you some time.'

He nodded and saw her downstairs and to the door.

'I want to be there, Cat.' He said what was on his mind. 'For the birth.'

'I know you do.'

'I'm not going to push it. I'm not going to demand or anything, I'm just telling you how I feel. I know I said that it didn't matter but it's starting to matter more and more to me. I don't think I'll be having any more children. I think this little one will be it.'

He went to touch her stomach and then remembered he couldn't, uninvited.

'You can,' Cat said, and he felt the little life when he was so cold today on the inside. Guilt dimmed a touch because how could this be wrong?

How could falling in love be wrong?

If, indeed, that was what he was doing.
'Go,' Dominic said. 'I need to think.'
And so too did she.

CHAPTER ELEVEN

'Dominic wants to be at the birth,' Cat said as Gemma finished examining her.

'What do you want?' Gemma asked.

'I don't know,' she admitted. 'I wish we had longer to work this all out...'

'You'd have had longer if you'd told him sooner.'

'Yes, well, I'm sure Dominic is thinking the same. I nearly told him about Thomas,' Cat admitted. 'And I know that at some point I'll have to. I'm just missing him more and more with each passing day. I'm missing all the things he missed out on and I know if I tell Dominic I'm going to start howling.' She looked up and she'd thought Gemma might be cross but her lovely friend had tears in her eyes.

She hadn't just delivered Thomas; Gemma had been his godmother. She had held him and loved him when Mike hadn't. Nigel too had been there, cuddling her baby and not grimacing at his imperfections, the way even her own mother had.

'I'm here for you, Cat,' Gemma said. 'As I am for all my mothers. If you don't want Dominic to be there, you can just say no and I'll see that it's enforced. If he is going to be there, he has to know you're going to be very emotional.' She gave her a smile. 'You finish up work this week?'

Cat nodded. 'Yes, I'm back here tonight for four nights and then I hang up my stethoscope for six months.'

'Are you okay to work?' Gemma checked.

'Is there a problem?'

'No,' Gemma said. 'If you feel up to it, that's fine. Your blood pressure is normal, everything looks good. You just look tired, Cat. I mean, really tired. I'm more than happy to sign you off for these last few nights.'

It was incredibly tempting but Cat shook her head.

'I don't think it's just the pregnancy that's causing sleepless nights,' she admitted. 'I'll see these nights through and then I'll concentrate on Dominic and me and try to decide what the hell I'm going to do about the birth.'

'Come on, then,' Gemma said. 'Let's get out of here. You're my last patient today and I need to get home. Nigel's got his French class tonight.'

'He's still learning French?'

'He is.' Gemma smiled as she put on her jacket. 'You know how we had to cancel the honeymoon because of my blood pressure with the twins? Well, he's determined we're going to have one. Though why he has to learn French to take me to Paris is beyond me.'

Cat waited as Gemma handed all the files over to the receptionist and wished her goodnight and then popped in to thank the midwife who had worked with her in the antenatal clinic today. They were out in the corridor and heading for home when Gemma stopped walking and turned to her. 'Friends now,' she said.

'Of course.' Cat frowned and then realised she was about to get a lecture.

'Let him in.'

'I don't know how,' Cat said. 'It's not just me. He never talks about Heather, or rarely. All I know is that she had a brain tumour, or rather tumours.'

'Why don't the two of you go away for a couple of days and talk things out while you're still able to?' Gemma suggested. 'You're thirty-five weeks now. There's still time. The best day of Nigel's life was seeing the twins being born. He cut the cords, he held them first...'

'I know,' Cat said, and then she smiled. 'Dominic's parents asked him to film it.' She thought Gemma would laugh but she just rolled her eyes.

'Tell me about it! I had a father ask if I could move a little to the left the other week so he could get a better shot.' They both laughed for a moment but then they were serious.

'If Dominic is going to be there at the birth, then he has to know about Thomas. If he's in the delivery room, he needs to be told that this baby isn't your first. He'll find out as soon as you get there.'

Gemma was right, Cat knew as she got ready to go to work that night.

She had a shower to wake her up and, thank goodness, Cat thought, she no longer had to worry about straightening her hair.

She massaged conditioner into the ends and then stood there for a good ten minutes, letting the water wash over her, holding her big fat belly and loving the life within.

He didn't get to do that, Cat thought as she looked down at the little foot or knee that pressed her taut stomach out.

Dominic didn't get to enjoy this simple, beautiful treasure of a moment.

Perhaps they should go away for a couple of days.

Talk.

Or not.

Just find out a little more about each other before the baby arrived and they attempt to co-parent. They were pretty much on opposite shifts at work, so they didn't really see each other there. Dominic was busy trying to get the house sorted on his days off and Cat was busy trying to catch up on sleep on hers.

She got out of the shower and combed through her hair. Everything was an effort and she wondered if she shouldn't have taken Gemma up on her offer to take these last nights off.

Despite it having been a nice clear day, it was cool and drizzling outside and the house was cold. She shivered as she crossed the hall and went into her bedroom. Turning on the light, she let out a small curse as the light bulb popped. Yes, she loved her high ceilings but it would be foolish to attempt to get out a ladder in the dark and climb it.

She'd ask Greg to come and change it for her.

She needed a Nigel, Cat thought, and then sat on her bed in the dark and surprised herself by bursting into tears.

No, she didn't want her own Nigel and she didn't want her brother dragging himself here on his way home from work just to sort out her light.

She wanted Dominic.

Cat laughed at herself, sitting there crying over a light bulb, but it was the very simple things that rammed the big things home.

She wanted the ease of asking him and didn't know whether she could or not.

It was time to find out.

She used the flashlight on her phone to choose what to wear, knowing that when she got to work she would be changing into scrubs and flat shoes. For now she grabbed her boots. She pulled out a small cami and the now well-worn paisley dress and went downstairs to put them on.

As she went to pull on her boots she remembered the hell of getting them off, but she'd deal with that later. Right now she couldn't be bothered to trudge back upstairs and rummage through her wardrobe in the dark.

Stop crying, Cat told herself as she drove to work, but the tears kept trickling out.

What the hell is wrong with you? she scolded herself. She parked in her usual spot and walked into Emergency.

There was Dominic, coming out of a cubicle, and he gave her a brief nod.

A colleague's nod.

Well, what did you want him to do? Cat asked herself. *You told him to stay back at work.*

But then he called her back.

'How come you're here?' he checked. 'You're not due to start till ten.'

'Oh!' That's right, she was on ten till eight instead of the more usual nine till seven. Her brain was so scrambled she kept forgetting the littlest thing.

Not at work.

At work she was fine but in all things domestic and mundane her memory was like a sieve.

She didn't tell him she'd mixed up her shifts. Instead, she just shrugged and walked into the changing room.

There was a knock at the door and Cat frowned and opened it.

'You've been crying.'

'Yes.'

'Can I come in?'

'It might look a bit odd if you're seen in the female changing rooms.'

'Not really. I'm checking on a heavily pregnant colleague who's clearly been crying.'

Cat went and sat on the bench as he came in and he stood against the closed door, like a security guard.

'So?'

She sat there for a moment. 'Can't I just be having a bad day?'

'Of course,' he said. 'How did the appointment go?'

Ah, that's right, Cat thought, he was worried about the baby, not her. 'All good,' she said. 'Head down. Gemma offered to sign me off work but only because I'm tired. Everything else is fine.'

'But you're here.'

'Yes.'

'And tired and teary.'

'My light bulb blew in my bedroom,' she said.

'You didn't try to change it?'

'I'm not stupid,' she answered quickly. 'No, I didn't try to change it.'

She looked up at him and he smiled, then spoke. 'You won't ask, will you?'

'I don't know if I can.'

'For God's sake, Cat, do you really think you can't even ask me that?'

'I know I can but what happens next time one blows? I mean, do I call you…?'

'Well,' Dominic said, 'from my light-bulb experi-
ence, when one goes the others tend to follow, so for the
next few weeks I will be on light-bulb duty.'

'Thank you.'

'Give me your key and I'll go and do it on the way
home and then drop the key back to you when I come
on in the morning.'

She looked in her bag to get it.

'Is there anything else?'

Say it, Cat.

She took a big breath.

'Do you want to go away?'

'Sorry?' Dominic's eyes widened, clearly taken back
by her suggestion.

'Well, I'm finishing up this week and I presume
you'll get some days off. I thought it might be nice to
get away before the baby comes along, sort out a few
things...'

'Separate rooms?' he asked, and she laughed.

'I haven't thought that far ahead.'

'I have,' he said, and came over. She thought it was
to take the key but having pocketed it he bent down.

'What are you doing?' she asked as he lifted one of
her legs.

'Helping you off with your boots,' he said. 'And it's
no to separate rooms.'

God, he was sexy. He lifted one leg and his eyes never
left her face as, far more easily than she ever could, he
pulled the boot off. 'But you said—'

'I know that I did but, as you know, I'm prone to
changing my mind.' He had her other leg up and was
pulling off the other boot, and if there had been a lock
on the door he'd have turned it.

'I think,' Dominic said, 'we should celebrate the one uncomplicated thing about us and have loads and loads of sex and then, maybe then, it might be a bit easier to talk...'

'Easier?'

'I can't think very straight at the moment.'

'Sounds like a plan,' she said. He was holding one leg and she was possibly in the least flattering position. Her dress gaped open, and she glanced down and thanked the sock gods that she'd lost them in the washing machine and her feet were bare.

She could see his erection and she was just as ready.

'I'll book somewhere nice,' she said, but Dominic wasn't waiting till next week.

'I could always arrange to come in late to work tomorrow,' he said. 'I'm on with Andrew,' he clarified, because she was frowning. 'Maybe I might need a little lie-down in your bed after I exert myself changing your bulb.'

'I might be a bit tired in the morning.'

'You won't be too tired, Cat.'

No, she wouldn't be.

Exhausted perhaps but as his hand stroked her calf she imagined it higher and she needed that now.

His pager was going off and it was possibly just as well, or they might be found in the most compromising of situations and their cover would be well and truly blown.

He leant over and gave her a kiss, a rough, wet one, and then pulled her to standing. Her stomach was hard and his hands were wild with possession but then his pager went again.

'You need to go,' she said.

'I need to come.' He grinned and gave her the briefest kiss but then he did the right thing and went to work.

Cat was way too early for her shift.

She could have let Dominic go early but was quite sure that he'd say no. Anyway, the thought of sitting down for an hour was terribly appealing so she made a mug of tea, took herself off to the break room and started to watch the news.

Her tea remained untouched, and within two minutes of sitting down she was out for the count.

Dominic popped in once to speak to one of the nurses about a patient he had in cubicle two and saw her there, dozing, and the dark smudges under her eyes.

He felt a bastard that in a few minutes he'd be waking her so that he could go home.

'Hey, Dominic.' Julia popped her head around the door. 'We've got a guy found unconscious outside a pub. He's talking now, but very confused...'

'Okay, I'll come now.'

His patent was in cubicle five.

'Hello, sir,' he said. 'I'm Dominic, one of the doctors on tonight.'

He was told, far from politely, where he could go.

'Okay, what's your name?' Dominic asked.

It was a swear word, apparently.

Dominic saw that the patient's blood pressure was high and when he checked it again, it was even higher.

'Does he have any ID with him?' Dominic asked, and Julia gave a worried shake of her head.

'He's got no phone, no wallet, nothing. I think he might have been mugged.'

Dominic couldn't smell alcohol on the patient, and while he had all the signs of being a belligerent drunk,

Dominic was very relieved to have been called promptly. He was growing increasingly sure that this man was suffering from a serious head injury.

'Come on, sir...' He tried to calm the man down and then glanced over to Julia. 'Can you call Radiology for me? And Mr Dawson.'

The patient spat.

'And an anaesthetist. I think we'll have to sedate him.'

Thank God Cat wasn't dealing with this, Dominic thought as he blocked a punch from the irate man.

He just wanted her safe at home.

CHAPTER TWELVE

CAT WOKE AND stretched and went to take a sip of her tea, then pulled a face when she realised it was stone cold.

She gave a small yelp when she saw that it was a quarter past ten.

Yes, she might need help with a light bulb but she didn't need help with her shifts at work. She had a long drink of water in the kitchen and then walked quickly to the department, retying her long hair as she did so and trying to convince herself that she wasn't too tired to work.

She heard a raised voice coming from a cubicle and frowned as somebody told Dominic incredibly inappropriately just where he could go and to please get away from him. Cat had this sinking feeling in her stomach as she recognised the voice.

'Sir.' Dominic's voice was crisp and calm. 'I'm very concerned about you. I want you to lie down. I'm going to get you a scan now. I believe that you have a serious head injury.'

He looked up as Cat came into the cubicle and she realised he hadn't been covering for her. He'd been busy trying to calm a very agitated patient.

'Nigel.' Cat went over and she knew instantly just

how serious this was. She was grateful that Dominic had recognised this wasn't a drunken man. This was gentle, kind Nigel, who at first didn't recognise even her.

'Nigel, it's Cat, you're at the hospital.'

He told her what she could do with that information and then he frowned as the familiar face came near him and he started to cry, angry, frustrated tears.

'Cat, what the hell is going on?' Nigel begged. 'Cat, help me.'

'We're going to help you, Nigel,' she said, and he finally lay down. She glanced up at Dominic. 'What happened?'

'We think he was mugged,' Dominic told her. 'We're just taking him to be scanned now. You know him?'

Cat nodded. She was trying not to cry herself as she held Nigel's heaving shoulders. 'This is my friend Gemma's husband. Nigel Anderson,' Cat said. 'He's thirty-two.'

'Any medical history?'

'I don't think so,' Cat said. 'This is nothing like him.'

'I get that,' Dominic said, his voice grim.

Nigel had given up fighting now. He had finally lain down but then he suddenly sat up and started vomiting.

'I'm going to go with him,' Dominic said. 'The neurosurgeon and on-call anaesthetist are meeting me there.' Joe, the porter, was running over.

Everything was under control, Cat realised. No, Dominic hadn't been covering for her. He'd been busy trying to give Nigel the acute care he needed.

'Call his wife,' Dominic said as he headed off with the patient.

For a moment Cat stood there, simply stunned, but

then she went to the nurses' station and pulled out her own phone.

She had made many difficult calls in her life, it was part of her job, but this would be, by far, the hardest she had made.

'Hey, Gemma,' Cat said.

'Cat!' Gemma answered, and then she must have realised the time, or perhaps heard the distress in her friend's voice, even though Cat was doing her best to sound calm. 'Is everything okay?'

'Gemma...' She took a breath.

'Is the baby...?'

Oh, poor Gemma, she was busy putting her doctor's hat on and now Cat had to put on hers. 'I've just started my shift. Nigel's been brought in.'

Gemma gave a shocked gasp. 'He's at his French lesson.'

'He was found in the street, Gemma. He has a head injury and is having a CT scan now.'

'Is he unconscious?'

'No,' Cat said, but she didn't want to offer too much reassurance because Cat knew that Nigel's condition was serious. 'He's very confused, Gemma.'

'How confused?'

'He was agitated.'

'Yes, well, he hates hospitals.' Gemma pushed out a nervous laugh. 'He doesn't even like coming in to have lunch with me and—'

'Aggressive,' Cat broke in, and she knew that in saying that Gemma would understand just how serious this was.

'How long will the scan take?'

'Not long at all,' Cat said. Fortunately, they had one

of the newest machines and the results would be in very quickly, though she was quite sure that Nigel wouldn't be returning to the department. He would, she guessed, be going straight up to either Theatre or ICU. 'Can you get someone to watch the twins and come here?'

'I'll call my parents.'

Cat looked up and saw that the light that meant there was an emergency in the radiology department was going off.

'Ask Gill to come in and watch them,' Cat said, referring to Gemma's neighbour. 'Andy can drive you in. I have to go now, Gemma.'

She loathed leaving her friend hanging. She knew the panicked state she had placed her friend in, but there wasn't time to wait for Gemma's parents. They were slow and annoying and would ask five hundred questions before they even started to reach for their car keys.

She rushed to the radiology department but the anaesthetist had arrived already and was intubating Nigel.

'He's got a small subdural,' Dominic explained. 'He started seizing and has just blown a pupil. We're going to race him up to Theatre.'

Nigel was now sedated and Dominic told her that the neurosurgeon had gone ahead to scrub as they started to move Nigel out. It was calm and controlled, the only panic in the room internal, and Cat looked at her friend's husband, perhaps the kindest man she knew, lying there fighting for his life.

She held his hand as they ran along the corridor. 'I'll look after Gemma and the twins,' she said to him, and at the elevators she gave an unconscious Nigel a very brief kiss as they went to move him in. 'You look after you and get well.'

She was breathless from her brief run and wanted to sit down on the cold tiled floor and cry but instead she pushed herself to turn around and head back down.

She could only guess at what was about to greet her.

'Where is he?' Gemma was frantic, running towards Cat just as she got back to the emergency department.

'I've asked at Reception…'

'Come in here,' Cat said, leading her to a small interview room.

'I want to see him now.'

'He's in Theatre, Gemma.'

Her friend simply crumpled. She just lost it.

She stood there and folded over and it dawned on Cat she had never seen Gemma anything other than calm before. Even when there had been a scare about the twins Gemma had remained upbeat and positive. Now, though, she couldn't even make it to a chair and it was Cat who held her up.

Thankfully, Dominic, back from taking Nigel to Theatre, came in and took over. He explained what was going on.

'They're operating on him now. He has a small subdural haematoma.' Dominic explained that Nigel was bleeding on his brain and that he had been rushed to Theatre to evacuate the bleed and relieve the pressure that was building. 'Mr Dawson is the one doing the surgery and he's one of the best.'

'He's brilliant,' Cat said.

'I don't understand what happened, though,' Gemma wept. 'He was at his French class.'

'It would seem he got jumped,' Dominic said. 'He had no wallet with him, no phone or ID. A passer-by found him lying down outside a pub. Luckily they called for an ambulance instead of just assuming he was drunk.'

'Nigel doesn't drink.'

'When he arrived here he was confused, he said that he needed to get home. His blood pressure was high and I arranged for an urgent CT scan. At that point Cat came on duty and of course she knew who he was. It all happened that quickly. He was drowsy during the CT and only at the last minute did he become unconscious.'

All poor Gemma could do now was wait.

'Cat will go with you to wait,' Dominic said, and Cat gave a grateful nod.

It was only as she walked out of the department that she started to realise she wouldn't be coming back to work until she was a mother.

Just as Nigel and Gemma had dropped everything for her when she'd had Thomas, it was time for Cat to do the same.

'Will you speak with Andrew and explain I won't be able to come in?' Cat said to Dominic.

'Of course,' he said. 'Just take care of your friend.'

She did.

It was the longest night.

Nigel came through Theatre and Mr Dawson was cautiously optimistic but he explained that Nigel would remain in an induced coma for the next forty-eight hours at least.

'I can't believe someone would do this for a wallet.' Gemma sat, holding his hand. 'He's got two little boys who need him. I need him.'

And Cat, who had sworn she'd never need anybody, knew what she meant.

She needed the breakfast that Dominic bought them

when he dropped in in the morning, having finished his shift.

She needed his support and she got it.

Her shifts were covered, Gemma's parents moved in to take over the twins and Cat went home at lunchtime and packed a bag for herself, then went to Gemma's and did the same for her friend.

When she got back to the hospital, they holed up as the world went on.

Just as Thomas had never been left alone, she and Gemma took turns to sit by Nigel's bed while the other slept. Even when his parents and brother visited, either Cat or Gemma were there.

Gemma trusted Cat to notice things she wasn't sure anyone else would, and it was the only way she'd consider getting some rest herself.

'How is he?' Dominic came into Cat's line of vision late on the second afternoon.

'The same,' Cat said. 'It's just a matter of waiting.'

'How's Gemma?'

'She's just gone home to check in on the twins. She's all upbeat and positive now. She's talking as if he's just had his wisdom teeth out.'

'How are you?'

Cat shrugged.

'Are you getting any sleep?'

'Some. Gemma and I have taken over one of the on-call rooms.' She looked up and smiled as her friend came back and Dominic spoke for a moment with Gemma and then left.

'How were the twins?' Cat asked.

'Teary and clingy. Mum and Dad keep asking when

I'll be back. I know that the twins are too much for them but what else can I do?'

'I can look after them,' Cat offered.

'I need you here, though.'

'Have you managed to get hold of your sister?' Cat asked. Gemma's sister was in the army and not immediately accessible.

'Finally, and she's asking for urgent leave and should be back in a couple of days.'

It was another long night and as Gemma slept through the morning part of it Cat sat with Nigel.

They were going to try to extubate him later and it was scary, to say the least.

'You have to be okay, Nigel,' Cat said. 'Your family needs you.'

'They do,' Gemma said, and Cat looked up and smiled at her friend. 'Thanks for being here.'

'Where else would I be?'

'And I must thank Dominic.'

'For what?'

'Covering all your shifts, bringing me decent coffee. He's gorgeous,' Gemma said, and took her seat by Nigel. 'I don't blame him for not saying he's a widower.' She took Nigel's hand. 'See, Nigel, you have to get well or I'm going to be getting loads of offers for sympathy sex…seriously,' she said to her comatose husband. 'I'll have all the single dads lining up to fix the car or the leaky roof. I'll have to fend them off.' She turned to Cat and smiled. 'Go and have a sleep. I'm going to talk dirty to my husband and remind him of all he'll be missing out on if he dares to leave.'

Cat slept.

The very second she lay down in the on-call room

she fell asleep and awoke with a jolt only when the door opened and there was Dominic.

'What's happened?'

'Good news, well, cautiously good.' He was holding a large mug and he waited for her to sit up, which was rather difficult to achieve, and then he handed it to her and brought her up to date.

'He was fighting the tube and they've extubated him.'

'Is he speaking?'

'No.'

'Has he opened his eyes?'

'No, but he responds to voices and is moving all limbs.'

'I should go…' Cat went to get out of the bed but he took her shoulder and pushed her back.

'No, no. Gemma's in with him. I've just come from speaking with her. Her mum's not well. Well, she's got a cold…'

'They're useless,' Cat hissed.

'I said that you'd go and watch the twins.'

'What did Gemma say?'

'She was relieved, I think.'

Cat let out her own sigh of relief. If Gemma was happy for her to go, then, really, things must be starting to look better for Nigel.

'I thought he was going to die,' she admitted.

'I know you did.'

For the past couple of days, since the moment she'd heard Nigel swearing and cursing, she had honestly thought he would die, or that the Nigel she'd known was gone.

Now there was hope that he was on his way back.

'Have your tea, then I'll drive you. There's no need to rush.'

'Are you working?'

'Just till five. Hamish worked last night and again tonight. I'm back in at nine tomorrow, but I can take half an hour to drop you at Gemma's.'

Cat nodded. She was way too tired to drive.

He sat on the edge of the bed and she looked at him—unshaven and exhausted—and she could see the strain in his features, and whether or not she was allowed to ask, she did.

'Is this hard on you too?' They both knew she was referring to his late wife.

'Yep.' He took a drink of her tea and then handed it back to her.

'Heather ended up in ICU and she hated me for it. She never said it, of course, but it was something she dreaded and not how she wanted it to be...' He didn't tell her any more and Cat sat there, not feeling slighted in the least. The sharing part was so incredibly hard at times. They'd been sort of thrust on each other by the baby.

That hurt Cat.

It was a niggle in her heart, a wound that gnawed.

That day when she'd thought he was cheating, instead of correcting her he had simply let her go—that was how much she had meant to him then, which made it hard to confide in him now.

'I'm going to see Nigel,' she said, 'and get Gemma's keys and things.' She looked around the room—in two days she'd accumulated quite a lot of stuff. Toiletries, clothes, towels...

'I'll pack it up,' he offered.

'Thanks.'

She buzzed and was let into ICU, where Gemma sat with Nigel's mum, but she stood up and gave Cat a hug.

'How is he?' Cat asked.

'Well, he didn't exactly open his eyes but he did sort of screw them up when I spoke to him,' Gemma said. 'He knows we're all here.'

Cat went over and gave Nigel a kiss. 'Hurry up and wake up,' she whispered into his ear, 'or she'll start talking dirty to you again.'

'He moved his eyes,' Gemma said. 'What did you just say?'

Cat laughed but she gave Nigel's hand a big squeeze. 'You keep getting better, okay?' She turned to her friend. 'Right, I'll go and watch the twins…'

'I feel awful, asking,' Gemma said, because she could see how exhausted Cat was.

'Please, don't,' Cat said.

'My sister will be here tomorrow, I hope.'

'It's fine. Just stay with Nigel and don't worry about anything else.' She smiled at Nigel's mum and headed out to where Dominic was waiting for her.

'How old are the twins?' Dominic asked as they walked to his car.

'Two,' Cat said.

'Good luck!' He smiled.

It felt strange, getting into a car with him again.

It was a different car from the one in Spain but there were coffee cups and papers and she looked around for a moment, remembering him taking her to Collserola and that morning.

She hadn't known him then.

She didn't really know him much better now.

Maybe Dominic was thinking the same thing, because

he turned on the engine and reversed out of his parking space and, just when she was least expecting him to, he told her about the very moment his world had fallen apart, the split second that he'd known everything was about to change.

CHAPTER THIRTEEN

'HEATHER WAS A VET,' Dominic said, and Cat turned and looked at him but didn't respond, and he remembered that he liked that about her—she didn't butt in or say unnecessary words.

'We met at university. She was crazy about animals. Horses, dogs, cats, cows…but mainly horses. She was a staunch vegetarian. She'd given up trying to get me to be one. Almost. Really, I think she would have been vegan by now.'

Still, Cat said nothing.

'We went out for years before we got engaged and it was a couple of years after that before we got married. I knew her very well, that's the point I'm making.'

He turned briefly and Cat nodded.

'One night she got up and, I don't know why, I came downstairs and I found her eating a steak sandwich. It was one of my steaks that I'd cooked and was taking for lunch the next day.' He managed a small laugh at the odd detail, yet it had been so very strange, just so completely out of character that he could remember to this day his confusion. 'Heather got all cross when I pointed out that she was eating steak, and said she was starving and she'd just fancied it and when she saw it in the fridge she couldn't resist it. I got that but it was bizarre, so unlike Heather. I thought maybe she had some sort of iron deficiency, or even that she was pregnant, perhaps. It was just a tiny thing that didn't make sense but then there started to be more and more tiny things. A couple of days later we had an argument that came from nowhere. She was furious about something and to this day I can't remember how it started. I just know that I had never seen her more angry. I knew then there was something very wrong.'

He gave a wry smile. 'It's very hard to say in the middle of an argument that I thought there might be something wrong with her... It would be like asking if she'd got PMT. But I knew that I wasn't arguing with her. I could reason with Heather but she was suddenly like a stranger. Anyway, she huffed off to bed and went for a sleep and woke up and was back to being Heather.'

The satnav announced they had reached their destination and Cat looked up and realised they were outside Gemma's, but she made no move to go in.

He'd told her more than she needed to know, but it was what he'd needed to tell her, so she understood.

'The row scared me and it must have scared her enough that she went to a doctor, who took her seriously. She called me at work and said she was about to have a head CT and would I come down.' He turned and looked at Cat. 'I knew,' Dominic said. 'I knew even before she had the scan and so did Heather. We went from normal to dying in one week.'

'No treatment?'

'Chemo,' Dominic said. 'But it was dire and really with little prospect, so after four rounds she pulled the plug. She always said we treated animals with more dignity than humans and she was very clear about what she wanted.'

Bizarrely, Cat thought, even though she wanted to know, she also wanted to tell him to stop.

She wanted to put up her hand and say, 'She died, I get it. I don't need the details. I cannot bear your pain,' but she sat there and looked at him and there wasn't a tear on his face, just a depth in his voice, and she understood now his quip about Gordon.

He wasn't mean at all—he was in agony and trying to hold on as he did what he had to.

Talk.

'Well,' Dominic said, and he reminded her a bit of Gemma, chatting away, as if she wasn't dying inside. 'We went on holiday, we thought we had a couple of months' grace. She wanted to go to Stonehenge. I don't know if it was a tumour making her wacky or just the way people go when they're dying—you know, the universe, God and living in the moment—but Heather got obsessed with sunrises. We were staying in a little cottage and I woke up one morning and she wasn't in bed. At first I thought she must have gone to get a drink or to the toilet but then I went looking for her. The front door was open. I drove around the streets and I met some guy who said he'd seen a woman being taken off in an ambulance...' He stopped talking then because there was a tap at the window and it was Gemma's mother, so cheery that the cavalry had arrived and she could go home.

Cat pressed open the window.

'Not now!' she snapped, and closed it again. 'Sorry about that,' she said to Dominic as Gemma's mum did an indignant, affronted walk back inside.

'The ambulance...' Cat said, and Dominic nodded, very glad Cat had told the woman to go. He just had to tell this story all in one hit.

'I called the local emergency department as I drove there but I never told them that she didn't want any active resuscitation.' He took a very big breath and his eyes silently begged her to say something.

'I doubt they'd have listened to someone calling in over the phone. I wouldn't have,' Cat said. 'I mean, I'd have listened and taken it in, but...' She shook her head.

'I didn't even tell them, though. I still feel like I let her down there.'

'You just weren't ready for her to die.'

'No, but I wish for her sake she had that morning. She got another three weeks and they were hell.' He gave her a grim smile. 'I could have told you all this at that lunch, nailed you to a wall like Gordon did...'

'You couldn't, though,' Cat said. 'I get why.'

Did she say it now?

Did she say, 'Well, guess what happened to me!'

Of course she couldn't. Anyway, Gemma's dad was heading towards them.

'I want to tell him to...' Dominic said, and that made her smile.

'So do I,' Cat said. 'But we won't.'

'No, we won't. I'm going to go back to work,' Dominic said. 'You're going to look after the twins and when you have time I'd like you to look up somewhere amazing for us to escape to the very second Nigel gets the all-clear.'

'I shall.'

'Go,' he said, 'and don't give me *that* look.'

'I shan't,' she said, and gave him a kiss on the cheek instead and then headed inside.

'Sorry about that.' Cat smiled at Gemma's very offended mum. 'That was a colleague from work and he'd just had some difficult news.'

Gemma's parents were already putting on their coats.

Cat soon understood that possibly it wasn't because she'd caused offence that they practically ran out of the house.

Two two-year-olds missing their parents and their routines.

Two two-year-olds who threw down their sandwiches because they didn't know how to say they liked them cut in squares, not triangles.

Two two-year-olds who were like wriggling eels in the bath as Cat knelt on the floor beside them that night.

Yes, they *all* needed Nigel, Cat thought as she got them into pyjamas and started to shepherd them down the stairs for some milk.

She wasn't a very good shepherd. One would go down, the other up, and she was too aching to carry them again.

'Daddy!' Rory squealed, when the key turned in the door.

'Mummy!' Marcus shouted, and the three of them stood there in slightly stunned surprise as Gemma came through the door.

'Gemma!'

Cat's heart just about stopped in terror as the twins thundered down the stairs and into their mum's arms. Gemma burst into tears and dropped to her knees and cuddled them.

'Is he…?'

'He's fine!' Dominic came in, carrying an awful lot of bags, only to look up and see Cat frozen on the stairs.

'Sorry,' Gemma said. 'I didn't meant to scare you. I just lost it when I saw the boys.'

'I wasn't expecting you,' she managed.

'Nigel told me to come and get some rest.'

'He's talking?'

'A bit.' Gemma nodded. 'Really, he's asleep most of the time but he's managing a few words and they've moved him out of Intensive Care.' Gemma, after her little meltdown, was trying to sound all calm in front of the boys but Cat could hear the wobble in her friend's voice. 'It's all looking good.'

'Thank God.'

'My sister should be here soon,' Gemma said. 'She's in a taxi on her way from the airport, so I thought I'd have a night to settle these two a bit before I head back there again.'

Cat stayed and helped her with the boys and Dominic sat half-asleep in a chair. Finally the twins looked as if they might be ready to crash.

Gemma and Cat carried them up and put them in their little beds and stood watching them for a while.

'I don't know how I could do this without Nigel,' Gemma said.

'Well, you're not going to have to find out.'

They went back down the stairs and Gemma told Cat to go home.

'You'll call me if you need me, though,' Cat said, her hands on her back, trying to stretch her spine.

'I shall, but once Angela gets here I should be fine. Thank you so much, Cat, and you too, Dominic.' As they went to head out Gemma called into the night, 'You'll call me if you need me, won't you, Cat?'

'I shan't be needing you for a while yet.' Cat laughed but Dominic saw the slight frown on Gemma's face.

'Cat...' Gemma strode towards them. 'You and Dominic need to sort this out.'

'Gemma!' Cat warned.

'No!' Gemma was practically shouting. Wrung out, emotional, she just spilled out her thoughts right there on the street. 'I just about lost my husband, and I'm telling you that there are moments in life that you can never get back, and if you don't let him in—'

'Gemma!' Cat broke in. 'We've got this, okay?'

'Well, make sure you have,' Gemma said, 'because life changes in a second.'

Then she burst into tears again and Cat and Dominic saw her back to the house.

'Sorry, sorry,' she kept saying.

'It's fine.'

Cat just about drooped in relief when she saw the taxi pull up and Angela get out.

Finally they got into the car and Cat let out a tense breath. 'God...'

'She's upset, she's tired,' Dominic said.

'She's interfering.'

And she knew she had to talk to him.

Just not tonight.

'Are you coming in?' she asked as they pulled up at her house.

'Well, if I do, it's for the night,' he warned, 'but that's only because if I sit down I won't get up again.'

'And me.'

'No wild sex,' he said. 'Because I don't want you to be disappointed.'

'You're safe.'

They were so tired they didn't even bother going through the motions of sitting down or making a drink. Instead, they scaled the stairs as if it were Everest.

'Is your back sore?'

'It's killing me,' Cat said. 'The twins wanted to be carried all the time, they were so clingy…'

They got to the bedroom and she went to turn on the light but, of course, it didn't work.

'You had one job to do,' she said, and they both laughed. It would keep.

She went for a shower and came back into her dark bedroom, where Dominic was already in bed. The street-light cast a slight orange glow and it was nice, so nice, to drop her towel and to get into her own bed, and she let out a lovely moan.

'That feels good,' she said.

'You have a very comfortable bed,' he commented.

'I know.' She sighed. Only, it didn't feel very comfortable tonight. She lay on her back and then turned and faced away from him.

'Rub my back.'

'I'm too tired,' he said, but he rolled over and obliged.

It wasn't sexual. It was intimate and blissful.

His fingers got right into the ache at the bottom of her spine and then moved up to the tight shoulders and then into her neck, and he remembered the spine that had greeted him on the day they'd met. He spoiled the thoughtful massage thing by getting a huge erection.

Cat kept feeling it, even as she tried to pretend not

to notice the brush of it against the back of her thigh now and then.

Then it stopped being a massage and his mouth came onto her shoulders and she closed her eyes at the bliss.

Not too tired at all, as it turned out.

His fingers came around the front as he kissed her neck and explored breasts that were twice as large as the last time he'd felt them.

He examined the changes. The thick, ripe nipples and then down to the taut swell of her naked stomach, and he got to feel the baby move and kick into his palm. It was a treasured moment.

Then his hand moved down to the curve of fuller hips and Cat let out a moan.

She wasn't too tired to move; she simply didn't want to. She liked it that all she had to do was nudge her bottom back a fraction to deliver her consent and he slipped in and his own moan told her it was bliss for him as he was drawn into that wet warmth.

'When I think of all those condoms I wasted on you,' Dominic said. They had deep, lazy sex and she turned her head and their tongues mingled for a very long moment. Then he got back to the easy task of making her come.

Very easy, because with each measured thrust she felt him tense more, and pressing back on him, giving in to him, the pleasure meant Cat was over and about to be done with. He came very deep inside her and she gripped him back and dragged out more. All tension left them.

'Now I'm comfortable,' Cat said.

'And me.'

They'd worked hard these past days for that long sleep.

But Dominic woke, as he once used to, just before sunrise.

He hadn't done that in months.

On this morning, though, Cat's long exhalation of breath and stirring of discomfort moved him from deeply asleep to half-awake and he lay there, feeling her stomach, which had been hard beneath his hand, soften.

Okay.

Light was starting to filter into the bedroom as he recalled Gemma's slightly odd demand that Cat ring her if needed, and he knew he was going to be a father today.

He already was, he thought.

From the moment in Oliver's when Cat had told him they were having a daughter he had become a father in his mind.

Soon he'd officially be one.

Thin rays started to stretch and strengthen and the black turned to grey and the room started to emerge. A chest of drawers, a large bookshelf and then grey dispersed and colour came in.

It was like waking up in some enchanted woodland.

There were trees, flowers, knotted wooden trunks and branches holding nests, and he half expected ivy to sneak across the bed and coil around them. He felt Cat's stomach tighten again beneath his hand and she stirred in discomfort.

'I lied to you,' he said.

Cat woke to those words and his kiss on her shoulder. 'When?'

'The second time we met,' Dominic admitted. 'I

didn't just happen to see the maternity leave position. I was already thinking of moving to London.'

'Not Spain?' Cat's brain was all foggy.

'I was thinking of moving to Spain, I almost was moving to Spain, but I couldn't quite get that weekend out of my head and I was wondering, before I cut all ties here, whether it might be worth...'

Cat lay there in silence as he continued.

'I regretted how it ended and I wondered if we stood a chance. I kept waiting to get over you but I didn't so I was looking at jobs in London. I was thinking of taking a temporary one before I moved to Spain and catching up with you to see...'

'See what?'

'If what we'd found that weekend still existed.'

Cat felt his hand stroking her stomach and his lovely long body melded with hers and, yes, what they'd found still existed.

'I haven't been honest with you,' Cat said, but tears tripped her words and he kissed the back of her head.

'That's okay,' Dominic said. 'You were stepping into my hotel room, not a confessional.'

Her stomach tightened and Cat stretched her legs out because it hurt, not just in her stomach but her back too and right down to her toes. 'Oh...' Cat breathed her way out of it. 'I think...'

'You are,' Dominic said. Her contractions were coming about five minutes apart.

'It's too soon.'

'You're thirty-six weeks, it's fine.'

'I mean, it's too soon for us,' she said, and started to cry. 'I was going to talk to you. I wanted to tell you things when we went away.'

'We've got ages to talk,' Dominic said. 'First labours take...' And he stopped then, halted at his own presumption as realisation hit.

'Second.'

She started to really cry.

It wasn't supposed to be like this.

They should be sitting in some lovely mansion, having afternoon tea, and she would be selecting a cupcake and mention Thomas, and Mike, oh, so casually and bypass the agony it had been. Instead, her stomach was in spasm and her knees were coming up and, ready or not, this baby was coming today.

'I want a bath,' she said. 'Oh, my God, we had sex...'

She was frantic for her bath and to arrive all clean and shiny in the labour ward.

No, it wasn't supposed to be like this.

He ran the bath, she rang the hospital and it was just as well she'd told him because the tired midwife asked if it was her first.

'No, it's my second.'

Dominic closed his eyes as he checked the water and then Cat came in.

'They said to come straight in.'

'Have your bath,' Dominic said. 'Your waters haven't broken...'

He helped her in and she got another contraction and from the strength and speed of them now she wasn't going to be sitting in the bath for very long. She looked at Dominic sitting on the toilet lid and there would be no Gemma delivering her. It would be a stranger. She had no choice but to confess how scared she was today.

And so she told him a little, about the happy person

she had once been and the baby and husband-to-be she'd had, and he sat, as she had for him, quietly.

She told him about the ultrasound and the Edwards syndrome and he didn't start demanding if she'd been thoroughly tested this time around, he just sat. And he didn't insist that it was unlikely to happen again and that his brilliant sperm couldn't possibly be at fault, he just sat.

'Thomas,' Cat said. 'Thomas Gregory Hayes.'

And he wanted to put his hand up and tell her to stop. *You had a baby, I get it.*

But they had to share themselves.

'Thomas, because I love the name. Gregory, after my brother, and Hayes because I didn't want Mike to be attached to him. He didn't want him...'

And still he sat there as Cat, angry, pregnant, lay in the bathtub.

'He's in the drawer.'

Dominic gave a slightly startled look as if she was telling him to go and fetch a dead baby or an urn of ashes from her bedside.

'His photo,' Cat said.

He went and fetched it and came back.

And, no, it wasn't how it was supposed to be. Where were her cupcakes, where was her cup of tea and something to distract her as he looked closely at her child.

Dominic sat on the loo seat as she breathed through another contraction, and when she finally opened her eyes it was to see the man who had told her with little emotion about the death of his wife crying.

He did not recoil in horror. He was looking at her son and then he looked at her and finally, only then, he spoke.

'A few weeks ago I couldn't imagine having a baby and now I'm sitting here trying to imagine how I'd feel if I lost one.'

Oh, my God! Cat was stunned. *He's crying!*

'Sorry, Cat.'

'It's fine.'

'No, I'm really sorry. I should be…'

What?

Stronger?

A touch more dismissive?

That he cried for her son and her loss meant the world.

'I wanted to get to twenty-five weeks,' Cat said. 'And then…' She told the truth. 'I didn't trust you enough to tell you about him.'

'I understand why you didn't.'

They trusted each other now. Their hearts always had but finally their minds had caught up.

'We need to get to the hospital,' she said, and as she stood her waters broke.

'Some one-night stand you turned out to be,' he said as he helped her out of the bath.

A drive that took twenty minutes at night was markedly longer at 7:00 a.m. and Cat was having visions of delivering at the kerb when thankfully the hospital came into view.

'Argh, I'm supposed to be working,' Dominic said, and made a very rapid call but then started to laugh.

'Poor Julia, she's really confused now. I just told her my partner's about to deliver a baby.'

They walked down the long corridor and gathered a few double takes along the way as some of the staff saw that snooty Cat was in her dressing gown *and* with the new sexy doctor.

That this was Cat's second pregnancy was on her chart, mentioned in every phone call made, and then the lovely doctor who came asked about Thomas as he went through Cat's notes.

'You had him at twenty-five weeks?'

Cat nodded.

'Normal vaginal delivery?'

'Yes,' Cat said. 'Well, it didn't feel very normal at the time.'

'Okay, I'm just going to take a look…' The doctor's voice trailed off as the doors opened and Gemma walked in.

'Thanks, Chand.' She smiled. 'This special delivery is mine.' And then she gave Cat a very severe frown. 'I told you to call me…'

'So you did,' Cat said. 'How did you find out I was here?'

'I told the ward that if you came in they were to let me know.'

'You knew I was going to have her.'

'Sort of,' Gemma said. 'But I was here anyway.' She started to pull on gloves. 'I couldn't sleep, I wanted to see Nigel.' Gemma looked over at Dominic and tested the water. 'Can you step out while I examine her, please?'

'He's staying.'

'I can have him removed.' Gemma grinned, delighted by the turn of events.

'There's no need for that,' Cat said.

'Has she finally told you?' Gemma asked, looking up at Cat's puffy face.

'Yep.'

'And so you know that this going to be very emotional for her,' Gemma checked. 'I mean, above and beyond.'

'I do.'

'How's Nigel?' Cat asked as Gemma pulled the sheet back.

'Talking,' Gemma said. 'He knows who I am, he knows the year we're in if not the month…he's doing really well,' she said as she examined her friend. 'As are you.'

Cat found out then that she was already fully dilated.

'Can you give me a push…?'

'I don't want to push.'

Oh, maybe she did.

'I'm not ready to push.'

'Yes, Cat, you are,' Gemma said, and nodded to the midwife, who was busily getting equipment out.

'Come on, Cat,' Gemma urged, when she lay there, fighting her own body and refusing to bear down.

'I can't.' She was starting to lose it. The lights were too bright, the voices too loud, and she'd never known pain like it. She wanted ten minutes to get used to the idea that her baby was on the way and when Gemma told her to push, right down into her bottom, she told her just what she could do with that notion.

'Come on, Cat…' Gemma's voice, Cat noticed for the first time, was really annoying. 'You can do this…'

'I can't,' she said.

She was scared to push, as scared as she had been the last time, but then Dominic spoke.

'Yes, you can,' he said, and she was about to argue when his lovely deep voice spoke on. 'You've done this before, Cat, you know what to do.'

He let Thomas in.

All the fear she'd had the last time, fear she still held on to, left, and she started to push her baby into the world.

She'd done this before, she had been a mother for seven years, just a lost one, but now the world was turning that around.

Gemma moved one leg back and Dominic the other. 'Just getting a better angle for the live-stream to my parents,' Dominic said, and that made her laugh.

'Come on, Cat…' Gemma said, and her voice wasn't annoying any more. 'Hold it…'

And there was a silence, a pause, and then she arrived. A little scrawny thing, very red and with a mass of black hair, she lay on Cat's stomach too stunned to cry, her little mouth open, her eyes screwed closed.

'Hey, kitten,' Dominic said.

'Don't,' Cat said. 'That's cheesy…'

But Cat and Dominic's kitten she was. Tiny and mewing and there, ready or not.

Dominic cut the cord and Cat just lay there, gazing down at her tiny, perfect baby and her funny-shaped head, little dark red lips. She had never been happier or sadder at the same time, because this was how it should be.

'It's okay…' Gemma was there when Cat folded. She'd known it was coming and she wrapped up her daughter and handed her to her dad, who had to juggle the two loves of his life. One arm full of baby, the other full of Cat as she cried for Thomas.

It was such a cry, one she had been dreading and the reason she hadn't wanted him near her for the birth. The midwife took away their daughter for a little while and

Gemma disappeared and she was alone with her heart and with him until the grief that would be present for ever faded enough to let life in.

Somehow they coexisted.

'Thank God I told you,' Cat said, because she couldn't imagine him not being here, not just for himself or their baby but for her.

'That's how I felt when I told you,' he admitted. 'Just relief.'

'Where is she?' Cat asked, when she peered out from the shield he had provided and wanted her little girl.

'Do you want her back in?'

She did.

Cat fed her for the first time and it soothed not just the baby but the baby's mum.

The midwife left and Gemma went to write up her notes and then it was the three of them.

'What are we going to call her?' Cat asked.

'I've no idea,' Dominic said.

For now she was Baby Hayes.

He didn't much like that.

When she finished feeding Cat handed their little daughter to her dad and she watched as he held her. She saw his expression falter and she knew that Heather was on his mind.

It didn't threaten her, not a bit. She knew he wasn't thinking that he wished Cat was Heather, more that Heather should have got to know this bliss.

'She'd be so proud of you,' Cat said, and let the other love in his life in, just as he had with Thomas.

'She would be,' he agreed, because Heather had known what a closed-off bastard he was and how long it had taken him to even commit to getting engaged. Yet here he was a dad and in love, not just with his baby but with the woman who'd given birth to her. Yes, she'd be so proud of him for pushing through, for showing up to each day and having the guts to fall in love again while knowing more than most just how much it could hurt.

Gemma came back in for a last-minute check before she headed back to visit Nigel.

'She's beautiful,' Gemma said. 'Just so gorgeous. I think I need to have another baby.'

'Don't tell Nigel that yet.' Cat smiled as her best friend got to hold her tiny daughter. 'You want to keep his blood pressure down.'

'I went over and told him you'd had a little girl and he smiled and said, "That's good." I'm starting to really think that he'll be okay.'

'Go and be with him,' Cat said. 'Thank you for being here today.'

'I couldn't not be,' Gemma said. 'I'm hardly going to miss out on delivering my own goddaughter...'

'Er...Gemma...' Cat said, and looked at Dominic. 'We haven't quite got around to discussing religion yet.'

'I don't even know how old Cat is,' Dominic said, and peered at Cat's observation chart and saw her date of birth. 'You're two years older than me!'

'Oh.' Gemma pouted, her doctor's hat clearly well and truly off. 'Well, bear me in mind when you do get around to it.'

'Tell you what,' Dominic said, 'if you can't be god-mother, how about you be bridesmaid?'

'Really?' Gemma beamed.

'Well, I have to ask her,' Dominic said, 'and then she has to say yes...'

'You'd better,' Gemma said, and handed back the baby, and when she'd gone Cat turned to Dominic.

'You don't have to marry me.'

'I know that I don't but I want to.'

'She can have your surname if that's what you want.' But, no, from the way Dominic was looking at her Cat was starting to realise that he loved her.

'I want you to have my name.'

'Not professionally, though,' Cat checked.

'Oh, yes,' Dominic said. 'I want my name on everything.'

'You are so completely not my type.'

'Well, you're not mine either,' he admitted. 'You stood outside that elevator in your lovely floaty dress, with your girlie curly hair, all blushing, shy and nervous…'

'Is that your type?'

'It was for a while.'

'Well, for your information, I wasn't shy and I wasn't nervous.'

'I know that now,' he said. 'You were turned on.' But then he was the most serious he had ever been. 'I never thought I'd do this again, Cat. I never thought I could get so lucky twice, but I have. So you're going to marry me, Gemma's going to be the bridesmaid and that's settled. Now all we have to do is choose a name for our baby.'

It was the best day ever.

And made more so by Dominic going out while Cat slept at lunchtime and returning with a very big ring. He then scratched out 'Baby Hayes' and changed it to 'Baby Edwards'.

'I don't think she's old enough to know,' Cat said.

'I know.'

They still couldn't decide on her name.

Her parents came, and then Greg and his wife and children.

A little later in the afternoon Eloisa was dressed in a little Spanish sleepsuit that had been bought a few weeks ago and had been sent along with a letter without judgment, just offering love.

And so they did live-stream with his barking-mad parents, though thankfully not the birth, and showed off their daughter to them and his sister, Kelly, as well as Cat's ring.

'She's beautiful,' Anna said.

'I know.' Dominic smiled. 'I think she looks like me.'

'I was talking about Cat!'

They were gorgeous!

And then a rather bemused Andrew popped in for a visit and did a double take when he saw Dominic sitting there by the bed and holding Cat's hand.

'I thought it was just a coincidence that your partner had gone into labour, Dominic. Then the rumours started flying and it would seem that they're true.' He just stood there bemused. 'You two?'

'Yep,' Dominic said.

'But why did you go to such lengths to hide it? You could have said at the interview.' Andrew frowned. 'Cat, you know it wouldn't have affected his chance at the role.'

Cat just smiled and chose not to tell Andrew that even she hadn't known he'd applied for the job and Dominic decided not to reveal he hadn't known for sure then if it was even his baby.

'I wonder,' Dominic said, when Andrew had left,

'what he'd have to say if he knew just what went on at the conference that the department sent you to.'

It was exhausting, being so happy.

So much so that when she'd fed her tiny baby again and put her down for a sleep Cat chose to take the midwife's advice to rest when the baby did. She didn't even notice that Dominic left, but awoke to the sound of the meals trolley. It rolled past her door.

'You're nil by mouth,' the midwife said, when Cat buzzed her to ask where her food was.

'Why?' Cat asked, but the midwife had gone.

She was starving and there was absolutely no reason for her to be nil by mouth, but then the midwife came back smiling, holding the door for Dominic, who was carrying a tray along with a big bucket holding champagne.

'Paella.' Cat licked her lips as he removed the lid and she saw the saffron rice and gorgeous seafood.

'Oh, and coffee...' She picked up the cup and inhaled. 'You remembered.'

'Of course,' Dominic said. 'I might not know an awful lot about you but I remember the little I do.'

Dinner in bed, her baby sleeping by her side and Dominic pouring champagne. It was time to get to know each other a whole lot more.

From the luxurious place of love.

EPILOGUE

Welcome to Gatwick Airport!

They were possibly the most frazzled bride- and groom-to-be ever.

On the plane the five of them took up a full aisle.

There was Cat on one end, Dominic on the other, Eloisa in her bassinet and Rory and Marcus creating havoc between them.

Nigel and Gemma were on a delayed honeymoon and were, about now, taking a leisurely drive from Paris to Barcelona. They would be there to meet them at the airport.

'Did you pack your pills?' Dominic checked, when they finally got off the plane. 'Because I'm not coming near you otherwise.'

'Oh, yes.' Cat nodded, very happy to have only one child.

The twins were adorable but, absolutely, Dominic agreed, they all needed Nigel.

And there he was with Gemma, smiling and waving. Cat's friend was very happy to see the twins and relaxed after a full week away from her beloved terrors.

She was also ready for a girls' night out before the big day, she told Cat as they walked to the car.

Cat and Gemma had a room booked for the night, her hen night, but for now Gemma was with Nigel, unsettling the twins and his routines, while Cat was in Dominic's room, sneaking in one last feed with Eloisa.

She was gorgeous, a smiley, happy baby who had her father's dark eyes and her mother's thick black hair.

'I *can* give a bottle,' Dominic said, holding his hands out to take her.

'I know,' Cat said. 'I just feel guilty,'

'Why would you feel guilty?' came Dominic's sarcastic response. 'I get the family buffet with Nigel and co. and you get to eat wherever you choose with adults and get as drunk as you please.'

'I know, I can't wait,' Cat said.

'Again she lies,' Dominic said. 'I assume it's not me and the family buffet you're feeling guilty about?'

'No.'

She *was* looking forward to her night out, she really was. She'd managed to breastfeed for only six weeks and now, at three months old, Eloisa happily took her bottle and Dominic often got up to feed her at night.

It was just…

'It's just…' Cat said. 'It's not just one night that I'm leaving her but two.'

'Cat.' Dominic was firm. 'If we hadn't got our problems sorted then about now, I might be having Eloisa to stay at my house for the night. And when you went back to work, there would have been no nanny, it would have been me.'

'I know.'

'And,' Dominic added, 'if you're worried about leaving her with my parents tomorrow, don't be. They are a bit odd but they will look after her as if she's made of glass.'

'I know all that.'

Cat loved his parents. She and Dominic had taken Eloisa to Spain when she was six weeks old and had stayed at the villa. Anna had been brilliant when Cat had been upset that her milk had dried up. She had been far more understanding about Cat's tears than her own mum would have been. Now they were back again just a few weeks later. Cat was looking forward to the next couple of weeks. After their wedding night they would stay at the villa again and she would get to know his parents better.

'I'd have brought her here without you,' Dominic pointed out. 'Not just yet, of course, but I always wanted her to be close to my parents. So just thank God we grew up and spoke to each other and that you're not crying your eyes out, driving back from Gatwick Airport, having just waved her goodbye.'

'Okay.'

'So go and enjoy your night out.' He smiled. 'And I'll see you tomorrow.'

She had the best night with her friend and her family. They went to the restaurant Dominic had first taken her to, and though she would tell him she'd had the paella he'd know she was lying.

'This chicken,' Gemma said, 'is amazing.'

'There's a lot of salt,' Cat's mum replied, and reached for a glass of water.

They laughed a lot, drank a bit much and danced into the small hours.

Well, Cat's mum and dad went off to bed but the two best friends had a brilliant time.

And then it was back to the hotel and she stayed up late into the night, chatting with Gemma.

'It was bliss,' Gemma said about their honeymoon. 'It was so nice to be able to talk to each other without being interrupted and to go for a walk without having to sort out hundreds of shoes.' She turned and looked over at Cat, who lay on her side in bed, listening to Gemma. 'I've got something to tell you.'

Cat both smiled and frowned. 'Well, I hope you're not pregnant, given the amount of champagne consumed tonight.'

'No, and I know both Nigel and I said never again when I had the twins, but we are going to try for another,' Gemma said.

'Yes!' Cat grinned. 'I knew you would.'

But that wasn't all.

'Remember when you joked about Nigel moving to France? Well, as it turns out, he wants to move there for a while and teach English.'

Cat's jaw gaped. 'And?'

'I want to take some time off with the next baby. Some real time off. I've loved working but before I know it the twins will be at school and I want some mummy time with them… So home might be France for a while.'

'It sounds brilliant,' Cat said, though she held on to news of her own until she could run it by Dominic.

'It does.' Gemma sighed. 'Though it's a terrible shame I did German at school! You know, a few months ago, as much as I said I'd give it every consideration, I'd still have freaked. We probably can't afford it, but…'

'You can't afford not to?'

Gemma nodded. 'Things were a bit tense between Nigel and I for a while,' she admitted. 'Nothing terrible but I was tired of working and felt I was missing out on the twins. But then his head injury happened and I thought I was going to lose him and, believe me, that changed an awful lot of things.'

Cat lay there remembering being with Dominic on the beach and his words—*'What seemed like the most terrible disaster at the time turned out to be a blessing.'*

There were so many blessings to be had.

'Spa day tomorrow.' Gemma broke the silence. 'I do love late weddings. There's ages to get ready and none of that hanging around between the service and party.' She looked at her friend. 'How come you chose sunset instead of sunrise, if that's when you two knew it was serious?'

'We just thought it would be easier to get everyone there in the evening,' Cat said. 'Greg isn't arriving till tomorrow.'

Gemma frowned but Cat changed the subject.

Just as Gemma hadn't told her till now about tense times with Nigel, she too didn't tell Gemma everything.

As she drifted off to sleep Cat thought about what sunrise had meant for Dominic and Heather, how she was quite sure that it had been that morning at Collserola that Heather had handed him over to Cat.

And sunrise was, for Cat, one of those times when you lay in bed with your baby feeding, and sometimes shed a tear for the one that you never got to feed.

Sunsets belonged to them, sitting outside in the garden, as Cat liked to now she had finally done it up. Sunsets were the time when she thought about Dominic driving home from work and the night to come, which was always precious.

Their wedding day dawned and Cat and Gemma awoke to breakfast in bed and then shared a spa day, getting massaged and oiled. Cat's hair was done and make-up applied and then late afternoon Gemma headed off to get Eloisa.

She was all smiles, blowing bubbles, happy to see

her mother, and together Cat and Gemma dressed her in
her little outfit and Cat's dad knocked on the hotel room
door and July was about to become beautiful again.

Oh, there were sad days in it but there were very
happy ones too.

They drove the short distance to Collserola.

'How far is it?' Gemma asked, once they were out
of the car and walking up the hillside, with Cat's dad
puffing behind.

'Nearly there,' Cat said, and then she saw her tribe
all waiting and she saw Dominic's smile when he noticed how they were dressed.

The bride and the bridesmaid both wore white.

Two broderie anglaise dresses. Cat's one had spent
three days at the dry cleaner's having grass stains removed, and two being expertly repaired, but she refused
to wear anything else for this very special wedding.

And, no, Gemma did not outshine the bride. No one
could for her smile was so wide as they stood at sunset at Collserola Park, with their families beside them.

Gemma held Eloisa, who was dressed in white
broderie anglaise too, and at three months of age was
going to spend her second night away from Mummy.

She was going to get to know her rather eccentric
grandparents on her father's side, of course.

Her rigid maternal grandparents were flying back
to England at the crack of dawn.

Still, they were here tonight and that was all that
mattered for now.

Or rather she and Dominic were all that mattered
right now.

He put a ring on her finger and Cat's eyes filled with
tears as he told her how much he loved her.

And then she put a ring on his finger, a finger that had worn one before, and Cat's eyes filled up again.

'I love you,' she said.

'I know you do.'

Their vows were said as the sun went down and life together carried on.

They had a party at his parents' villa.

Greg's children swam in the pool and Nigel took the twins inside for a sleep.

Cat dived into the paella and looked up to see Anna holding her granddaughter and smiling down. Kelly asked her something and Anna stood and handed little Eloisa over to her husband, who took the baby with a smile.

It reminded her of that precious time with Thomas when he had never been put down and had been surrounded only by love.

'She'll be fine,' Anna said, bringing out a tray of desserts and placing them on the table.

'I know she will.'

They had their priorities right, Cat thought, glancing at her own parents, who were both checking their phones.

She thought about the letter James and Anna had sent her, inviting her, with or without Dominic, into their home. Cat understood better now why Dominic would have fought, legally if he'd had to, to have his parents in his daughter's life.

It hadn't come to that, though.

They partied into the night and then it was time to head back to the conference hotel for Dominic and Cat, though to the luxury suite this time.

'She's sound asleep,' Dominic said as they crept in to whisper goodnight to their daughter.

'How lucky are we?' Cat said, remembering how it might have been.

Dropping the baby off.

Picking her up.

Doing this apart, instead of together.

'Come on,' he said. 'I guess we have to go and do what newlyweds do now.'

'I suppose.' Cat sighed.

They couldn't wait!

They left the people they loved and were driven to the hotel.

They walked through the foyer. 'Do you want a quick drink at the bar?' Dominic nudged.

'No.'

The elevator door opened and together they stepped in and this time there was no hugging the wall and wondering where the night might lead.

It was straight to his arms and a blistering kiss and it would be straight to bed, except Cat had something on her mind.

'I've been thinking,' Cat said as they stepped into the suite and Dominic poured champagne.

'Have you?'

'How's my job?'

'Do we have to talk about work tonight?'

'Please.'

'It's busy,' Dominic said. 'Are you still thinking about job-sharing with me?'

Cat shook her head. It was something they'd both considered but Cat had other plans.

She loved him.

No question.

'I was thinking of selling my house,' Cat said, which made sense, given they spent most of their time at his.

'I'm going to make a nice profit. Enough to maybe take a year off work.'

'What are you going to do?' Dominic asked. 'Renovate mine?'

'No.' Cat laughed at the hope in his voice and she closed her eyes at his kiss and his hands that were, more tenderly this time, removing her dress. 'I think I want to learn Spanish.'

Dominic stopped in mid-kiss.

'Er...why?'

'I'd like to be able to speak with the locals,' Cat said. 'You said you wanted to spend some time here.'

'I did.'

'Then do,' Cat said. 'You've already upended my life, so why not a little bit more?'

'When did you decide this?'

'I started thinking about it last time we were here. I can see how much you love it and I think it would be amazing to live here for a while, and then...' She thought of life here with him and smiled when she thought of her best friend just a leisurely drive to Paris away, and she gave a small shrug. 'Who knows?'

She loved him and love deserved careful consideration at times.

He had made her so happy, had given her back her dreams, and she wanted to make all his come true too.

She had been far too cynical about men, about love, about hope.

'You're sure?' he checked.

She was now.

Absolutely, Cat was sure of this love.

* * * * *

MILLS & BOON®
Hardback – October 2015

ROMANCE

Claimed for Makarov's Baby	Sharon Kendrick
An Heir Fit for a King	Abby Green
The Wedding Night Debt	Cathy Williams
Seducing His Enemy's Daughter	Annie West
Reunited for the Billionaire's Legacy	Jennifer Hayward
Hidden in the Sheikh's Harem	Michelle Conder
Resisting the Sicilian Playboy	Amanda Cinelli
The Return of Antonides	Anne McAllister
Soldier, Hero...Husband?	Cara Colter
Falling for Mr December	Kate Hardy
The Baby Who Saved Christmas	Alison Roberts
A Proposal Worth Millions	Sophie Pembroke
The Baby of Their Dreams	Carol Marinelli
Falling for Her Reluctant Sheikh	Amalie Berlin
Hot-Shot Doc, Secret Dad	Lynne Marshall
Father for Her Newborn Baby	Lynne Marshall
His Little Christmas Miracle	Emily Forbes
Safe in the Surgeon's Arms	Molly Evans
Pursued	Tracy Wolff
A Royal Temptation	Charlene Sands

MILLS & BOON®
Large Print – October 2015

ROMANCE

The Bride Fonseca Needs	Abby Green
Sheikh's Forbidden Conquest	Chantelle Shaw
Protecting the Desert Heir	Caitlin Crews
Seduced into the Greek's World	Dani Collins
Tempted by Her Billionaire Boss	Jennifer Hayward
Married for the Prince's Convenience	Maya Blake
The Sicilian's Surprise Wife	Tara Pammi
His Unexpected Baby Bombshell	Soraya Lane
Falling for the Bridesmaid	Sophie Pembroke
A Millionaire for Cinderella	Barbara Wallace
From Paradise...to Pregnant!	Kandy Shepherd

HISTORICAL

A Mistress for Major Bartlett	Annie Burrows
The Chaperon's Seduction	Sarah Mallory
Rake Most Likely to Rebel	Bronwyn Scott
Whispers at Court	Blythe Gifford
Summer of the Viking	Michelle Styles

MEDICAL

Just One Night?	Carol Marinelli
Meant-To-Be Family	Marion Lennox
The Soldier She Could Never Forget	Tina Beckett
The Doctor's Redemption	Susan Carlisle
Wanted: Parents for a Baby!	Laura Iding
His Perfect Bride?	Louisa Heaton

MILLS & BOON®
Hardback – November 2015

ROMANCE

MILLS & BOON®
Large Print – November 2015

ROMANCE

The Ruthless Greek's Return	Sharon Kendrick
Bound by the Billionaire's Baby	Cathy Williams
Married for Amari's Heir	Maisey Yates
A Taste of Sin	Maggie Cox
Sicilian's Shock Proposal	Carol Marinelli
Vows Made in Secret	Louise Fuller
The Sheikh's Wedding Contract	Andie Brock
A Bride for the Italian Boss	Susan Meier
The Millionaire's True Worth	Rebecca Winters
The Earl's Convenient Wife	Marion Lennox
Vettori's Damsel in Distress	Liz Fielding

HISTORICAL

A Rose for Major Flint	Louise Allen
The Duke's Daring Debutante	Ann Lethbridge
Lord Laughraine's Summer Promise	Elizabeth Beacon
Warrior of Ice	Michelle Willingham
A Wager for the Widow	Elisabeth Hobbes

MEDICAL

Always the Midwife	Alison Roberts
Midwife's Baby Bump	Susanne Hampton
A Kiss to Melt Her Heart	Emily Forbes
Tempted by Her Italian Surgeon	Louisa George
Daring to Date Her Ex	Annie Claydon
The One Man to Heal Her	Meredith Webber

MILLS & BOON®

Why shop at millsandboon.co.uk?

Each year, thousands of romance readers find their perfect read at millsandboon.co.uk. That's because we're passionate about bringing you the very best romantic fiction. Here are some of the advantages of shopping at www.millsandboon.co.uk:

* **Get new books first**—you'll be able to buy your favourite books one month before they hit the shops

* **Get exclusive discounts**—you'll also be able to buy our specially created monthly collections, with up to 50% off the RRP

* **Find your favourite authors**—latest news, interviews and new releases for all your favourite authors and series on our website, plus ideas for what to try next

* **Join in**—once you've bought your favourite books, don't forget to register with us to rate, review and join in the discussions

Visit **www.millsandboon.co.uk**
for all this and more today!

MILLS_WEB_HB